Books By Alice Hornbaker

**Preventive Care: Easy Exercise
Against Aging (Drake)**

Adoption – Who Needs It? (A children's book)

WOLD

IN CINCINNATI

Alice Hornbaker

iUniverse, Inc.
Bloomington

iUniverse books may be ordered through booksellers or by contacting:

iUniverse
1663 Liberty Drive
Bloomington, IN 47403
www.iuniverse.com
1-800-Authors (1-800-288-4677)

ISBN: 978-1-4502-9021-0 (sc)
ISBN: 978-1-4502-9020-3 (hc)
ISBN: 978-1-4502-9019-7 (ebook)

Library of Congress Control Number: 2011901451

Printed in the United States of America

iUniverse rev. date: 2/25/2011

This novel is dedicated to Joe Hornbaker, Holly Hornbaker, Chris and Tammy Hornbaker, Elzie Barker, Anne Clark and Editor Blair Kenney

CONTENTS

PROLOGUE ix

CHAPTER I – The Fire 1

CHAPTER 2 – The Aftermath 7

CHAPTER 3 – Jennifer Patricia Stein 13

CHAPTER 4 – WOLD 20

CHAPTER 5 – Sylvia Biggs 23

CHAPTER 6 – Carolyn Armstrong 37

CHAPTER 7 – Jim Ticknor 45

CHAPTER 8 – Bob Redding 56

CHAPTER 9 – Volunteers 61

CHAPTER 10 – The Whisperer 66

CHAPTER 11 – Intrigue 69

CHAPTER 12 – A Visitor 78

CHAPTER 13 – Vengeance 87

CHAPTER 14 – The Set Up 92

CHAPTER 15 – No Show 97

CHAPTER 16 – Lover Come Back 100

CHAPTER 17 – Three To Get Ready 104

CHAPTER 18 – A Puzzle 110

CHAPTER 19 – Bookkeeping 116

CHAPTER 20 – Lana Knows 124

CHAPTER 21 – Heroes 137

CHAPTER 22 – To Catch A Thief 153

CHAPTER 23 – Retribution 158

Epilogue 174

PROLOGUE

Long before women's liberation, reporter-want-to-be Jennifer Patricia Stein suffered from gender discrimination.

"You can't do that" she heard throughout her childhood, from male voices. Rather than wound her, it made her strong, determined, and allowed her to morph into a successful journalist.

As a high school freshman, Jennifer wanted to work on her large high school's newspaper staff as a sports reporter.

"You can't do that," her English teacher and staff advisor, a male, told her, "You are a girl. We don't allow girls to cover our sports."

She did, though, the hard way.

Sitting in the field seats watching a high school baseball game once after school, a line drive struck her in the head. Knocked her out.

She survived and demanded her account of what happened be printed in her own words in the high school newspaper. The male faculty advisor gave in, thinking perhaps her family might sue if they did not.

After that incident that paper's male advisor allowed Jennifer to cover some track and field events. But off limits to her were baseball and football. Only male teens could do that. Girls, they told her, knew nothing about those games.

They didn't know Jenny was the only child of a man who longed for a boy to talk baseball to and instead got Jenny. So he taught her everything about the sport, took her into the bleachers to watch season after season of the Cincinnati Reds play.

He taught her how to keep an official score card, explained to her the strengths and weaknesses of each player in the daily lineup, even bought her a Reds' baseball cap which she seldom took off growing up.

Jennifer went off to college determined to become a collegiate sports reporter, covering all sports, women and men.

"You can't do that," the male head of the journalism department told her when she signed on to be the only female in that department. "Women don't cover men's sports."

Jennifer wrote about women's sports, but followed all the teams. Then she briefly dated a fellow student who was a star on the college boxing team.

One boxing event Jennifer attended was a match between her friend and another boxer who was called "the knock-out king." He floored Jennifer's friend in the first round. She rushed to follow the dazed young man and his entourage down to the locker room.

"You can't go into the men's locker room, Jenny," the boxing coach said, pushing her aside.

"But I'm covering it for our Tiger Press," she lied.

The empathetic coach who admired Jennifer's determination spoke those same hated four words that fueled Jennifer's life, "You can't do that." He added, "You are a girl." But seeing her disappointment, he added, "Your friend will be fine, though. Go back to the arena."

After graduation and working on a metropolitan newspaper Jennifer again asked that sports editor to allow her to cover some sports along with her assignments for the women's department.

"Women don't cover sports," the sports editor said, after he stopped laughing long enough to spit out those words.

Fast forward.

The college boxing coach she so admired in college had a stroke. His wife called Jennifer while she was working on the local newspaper in the city. "Jennifer, my husband is recovering from a stroke at the hospital. He asked to see you. Any chance you might visit him this weekend?"

That next Saturday after the call Jennifer was at the coach's hospital bedside.

"You were so persistent trying to cover sports in college I remembered you. I now read your delightful human-interest stories in the newspaper. That's your forte, Jenny. Tell the public stories about real people whether they are sports figures or presidents or the local bridge club. I have a few stories I'd love to tell you about college sports in general, and boxing in particular. Interested?"

"Yes, sir!"

Jenny's coach stories ran as a series under the banner, "Confessions of a college boxing coach." That garnered some real assignments later on from her newspaper's sports editor --- people stories such as one featuring the star quarterback on Jennifer's alma mater's college team who overcame polio to play sports again.

Jennifer married and continued her career as a reporter for years, winning many awards for her feature stories about people, good, bad, and ugly. She then branched out to become a freelance magazine writer for national magazines from the Sunday New York Times to People to a brief stint at a infamous tabloid where it was rumored had Mafia connections.

Her teen daughter Trisha, asked, "Mom, why do you work so hard to tell other people's stories? Why don't you tell your own?"

Jennifer smiled. "I do, every time one of my stories goes into print. It says to all those doubters, yes I can. And I have."

CHAPTER I – The Fire

Jennifer Patricia Stein (professionally known as J.P. Stein) couldn't believe the office she stepped into on the 20th floor of the Star-Times newspaper building. She'd zoomed up so rapidly she thought she'd lose her breakfast.

Publisher Tyson Cook's ultra modern office featured floor to ceiling windows, displaying an all-grown-up Cincinnati in 1976 with high rising buildings and a river view. It was far different from more than twenty years ago when J.P. left conservative Cincinnati.

Several black pillows highlighted the publisher's stainless steel and white leather furniture. On the floor were large white fur rugs. One solid wall featured a bright Henri Matisse reproduction of "The Plum Blossoms." One red rose was in a large crystal vase on the publisher's huge glass and steel desk. The place was a shrine to the future, with flair.

"So this is journalism today?" the former reporter J.P. thought, her feet sinking into the area rugs as she entered for her job interview. A far cry from her first job reporting from inside one large, messy, smoked filled big room where reporters drank heavily, smoked incessantly and reported to an all male editorial

staff. As for that publisher's ancient suite, it was conservative, full of antiques, stuffy.

J. P.'s heart pounded today in anticipation of working for a youth-oriented metropolitan newspaper that embraced high technology.

Problem though: she was from that dinosaur age.

Managing editor Andy Stokes burst into publisher Tyson Cook's 20th floor office waving his hand toward the television set.

"Turn on the TV, Ty," he commanded his boss. "For God's sake, Lana Koppler is missing!"

He ignored Jennifer Patricia Stein, or J.P., sitting there, wide-eyed. He had just interrupted her unfinished job interview with Cook to join the Star-Times staff as its chief feature writer.

"You, too, J.P." he ordered Jennifer. "Pay attention. I want you over there, too."

There? Where? Bewildered, Jennifer looked up to see on the TV screen pristine grounds as green as artificial turf. Fire trucks and emergency vehicles were strewn everywhere. A TV reporter described the scene.

Andy directed his explanation to Cook. "Our reporters called in that Lana Koppler lives up in that fifth floor penthouse there, see?" His finger scanned the screen. "See? Up there, where that smoke is? It's mostly just that now. But what is news is Lana's disappearance. She got out, we assume, but no one has seen her since."

For J.P.'s benefit he added, "That's Pleasant Hill Farm retirement community, where some of our retired rich and famous Cincinnatians live. Its most famous occupant, Lana Koppler, is 90, and she hasn't been located. I want you at that campus to find her and get a quote. You're comfortable interviewing elders. Our young reporters are not. That's what you do best. It's that simple."

Turning back to Cook he said, "I'm betting my next week's pay that J.P. here, your new hire, might get an interview with Lana our young reporters won't, providing Lana's not dead. It would be an exclusive for us to have her quote."

"Our new hire?" That's all J.P. heard that through the madness of this scene. But was this notorious bad-tempered managing editor Andy Stokes insane? J.P. hadn't finished her job interview. Cook hadn't hired her.

But Cook apparently agreed with Andy.

"Brilliant idea Andy. J.P., yes, you're hired. We'd decided that before you arrived today. Your credentials are impressive. So go with Andy. He's on to a great idea."

"Get up. Let's go," Stokes commanded Jennifer, obviously used to being immediately obeyed by reporters.

Stokes grabbed her left arm. "Come with me."

They descended down from the 20th floor to the fourth so fast Jennifer felt queasy. Heights made her uncomfortable, too. Stokes pressed and held down the elevator button to allow no stops before reaching the fourth floor, and a waiting Sylvia Biggs, Leisure Plus editor and soon to be Jennifer's new boss.

J.P. wondered if this is how they treat all potential new hires.

The elevator doors opened. Sylvia Biggs took Jennifer's right arm as though she were a package to be delivered, announcing, "I've got her now, Andy," waving him off with such authority that the managing editor retreated to his office. Interesting, J.P. thought, a mere editor dismisses the managing editor. How come? What power does she pack?

J.P. stared into a pair of intense blue eyes of a woman dressed in an impeccably tailored white linen suit who could pass for a movie star, a young movie star. In this year of 1976 and at age 49, Jennifer felt ancient. Everyone else around her seemed so young. Suddenly the "youth oriented" pitch in today's professional society stung her.

"I know this is a hell-of-a-way way to start off a new job, J.P.," Sylvia apologized, trying to calm her new hire, "but management met yesterday and decided to hire you today to specialize in stories on aging, which you've already done so well as a freelance magazine writer.

"Lana Koppler is The Farm's famous nonagenarian and she's missing in that fire. But knowing her she's probably just sitting out this emergency sipping on a martini in The Farm's campus bar. She doesn't give press interviews. What Andy hopes is maybe with your magic touch with elders perhaps you'll succeed."

Both went into Sylvia's glass enclosed office that anchored the Leisure Plus's smoke-filled newsroom. Some things never change, J.P. thought.

"Here, take this package." Sylvia thrust a large envelope toward Jennifer. "It's got everything you need to drive over there to Pleasant Farm and see what you can find out about Koppler. Your press pass is there. Our reporters at the fire has been alerted you're new and coming over. You probably won't be able to talk to Lana, assuming she's hiding out somewhere, but in case you do get lucky and get a few quotes from that grand dame it would make a great sidebar to our news stories."

Sylvia took a breath. "This is a breaking story, so hustle."

J.P. was subject to headaches under stress since the divorce. One crept up on her now. She rejected it and thought, "Please God, not now. This big chance. I need this damn job."

She grabbed the bag Sylvia held out and said; "I've been away from Cincinnati for 20 years and only relocated here a couple of weeks ago. I've never heard of The Farm, much less how to get there."

Sylvia waved her off with "Don't worry. The Farm is new. So I put instructions how to get there into your package. Your hometown hasn't changed that much. Just more grown up. Also check in at The Farm's little FM radio station called WOLD. Its format is nostalgia music only so it won't broadcast this hot news. But there's a bright station manager there

5

who might find a way to help you contact our reclusive Lana. So, go."

CHAPTER 2 – The Aftermath

None of the luxurious apartments or cottages at The Farm could compare to Lana Koppler's place. Her huge penthouse was on one building's top floor. The other four floors each held had two apartments. Lana insisted on having, loft-style, the entire fifth floor bringing with her as much as she could from her famous mansion.

Lana's space included a personal art gallery, antiques, a fitness area for her daily treadmill "walks" that still happened at age 90, and a study that stunned others who first saw it. All the study's walls and especially the entire ceiling were covered with black and white glossy publicity photos autographed to Lana. Frank Sinatra smiled down from the ceiling, as did Tony Bennett. There was an autographed photo of Sophie Tucker, George Burns. Grace Allen, Rosemary Clooney, Bob Hope and Bing Crosby. Lana's kitchen was far larger than in other apartments as her housekeeper, Friday, demanded a large working space for Lana's frequent entertaining.

On day two of her new job J. P. made a sharp left turn off the elevator to the former women's department, renamed Leisure

Plus. Its newsroom layout featured many small cubicles, resembling a build-a-better-mousetrap design. A glass partition at the end was Jennifer's destination—to talk with her editor boss. A sign on the door said "Sylvia Briggs, Leisure Plus editor."

Finally, J.P. thought, some answers after yesterday's madcap day where she observed a minor fire and actually met The Farm's prime resident, multi-millionaire philanthropist Lana Koppler, who J.P. discovered seemed a lot younger in person than 90, or at least in mental acuity.

J.P. found and first observed Lana inside radio station WOLD's largest studio busily trying to brush off those determined to aid her during her emergency visit inside WOLD's studios.

With practiced authority Lana dismissed reporters, a solicitous young giant Farm security guard determined to guide to her back up to her penthouse, and various firemen who tried to be of help to the famous woman.

J.P. noted Lana's rather frail-looking body moved well in her flowing chiffon summer dress that screamed expensive. Unlike many elderly women J.P. profiled, Lana wore makeup and her hair was styled.

Now Lana ordered everyone to back off as she prepared to return to her penthouse without all the unwanted assistance. She had taken refuge in WOLD's studios after firemen evacuated her entire building. In deference to the famous woman the fire chief came in to announce an all clear and say the elevator was again working. "Damage Mrs. Koppler, "was quite minimal."

Keenly aware of the deference shown to Lana, J. P. introduced herself first to station manager Carolyn Armstrong, who then took Jennifer to Lana. For reasons only known to Lana, J.P. was graciously acknowledged and granted a brief interview while all others around were shooed off.

By news instinct J.P. had first sought out Carolyn to help locate the missing Lana. A lifetime of gut feelings guided J.P. to the right news source. To her surprise, Lana was safely there and being patronized by its staff. Carolyn introduced Jennifer to Lana. To everyone's surprise, J.P was invited to sit down with her.

As it turned out, Carolyn's mention of Jennifer's name clicked with astute and voracious reader Lana Koppler.

"I read that wonderful piece you did sometime ago for some magazine on that Jewish grandmother who survived the Holocaust as a child," she told J.P. "It touched me."

J.P was close to speechless, a first for the aggressive reporter. That Holocaust story was a memorable one for her as well and it won an award. But now the reclusive Lana remembered it, so she "granted" J.P. a small interview because of it.

Lana said, "I love children and I felt deeply for that grandmother who as a child of 12 became a Nazi sex slave. As I remember she'd been singled out of lineup of Jewish women prisoners, then her Aryan-looking blonde hair and blue eyes gave her status. The other children and women were ordered to the ovens but she was saved. You told her story so well I cried."

J. P. remembered. That story was almost too painful to write about. Yet here sat the famous Lana Koppler who remembered J.P's old story and got her this hard-to-get interview.

WOLD's largest radio studio was filled with volunteers and staff. J.P. noted before she sat down that Lana scolded the young security guard who aggressively attempted to escort Lana back to her penthouse. J.P. overheard the guard say, "We want to make sure that new security system you installed wasn't damaged by the fire. I'd like to check it out and help you back up."

Lana snapped back, "Sonny, that's my job, not yours. I may be 90 but I can climb those five flights of stairs to get home alone if I must. I have done it a number of times. Only today I don't want to. I have help."

She brushed him away with her hand.
Or dismissed him, J.P. thought, like royals do subjects. This crowd obviously catered to Lana.

Yet graciously, J.P. thought, the famous philanthropist answered a few of J.P.'s questions. But very few. Then she arose to take the arm of her doting housekeeper-companion named Friday, a chunky woman junior to Lana by at least thirty years. As elegant and stylish as Lana was, Friday was plain. But the way she attended to her boss and patron convinced

J.P. there was a real devotion. Note J.P. wrote to herself: "Lana Koppler deeply cares about other people. She is no rich snob."

Lana abruptly cut off the interview, stood up, anxious to depart. The fire chief excused himself to return to tell his crew Lana Koppler was fine. Lana and Friday left arm in arm, with J.P thinking, what an odd couple they seemed to be. Lana is the mama bear and beside is her docile cub. In any emergency, despite differences in their age, it's obvious who leads and who follows.

The fire's cause, Jennifer found out later, was faulty wiring. The sprinkler head in the kitchen quickly doused the flames, but triggered the alarm on cue.

Lana's building elevator serviced all floors in her building. Pleasant Hill offered a wide variety of housing on its 100-acre campus, from plush apartments to large three and four bedroom cottages, all tailored to each occupant tastes. Most cottages were built cul-de-sacs spaced out across the campus. Those who preferred apartment living also had choices of custom interior designs.

Actually The Farm looked like any suburban wealthy neighborhood with an over abundance of trees and shrubbery.

Lana's fifth floor was reminiscent of a city loft. WOLD station manager Carolyn Armstrong told J.P that Lana had worked with The Farm's CEO Bob Redding to design the apartment to fit her own personal taste, adjusting blueprints to accommodate her every need, right down to a secret wall safe.

All apartments and cottages had sprinkler heads in every room. Fires were practically non-existent in the five years since The Farm was built. The fire chief told J.P. no one who lived on The Farm's grounds would ever die of burns. More likely they'd drown from the over abundance of sprinklers. That's why damage to Lana's place was so small.

J.P. got her news quotes from Lana and turned it into a sidebar to accompany the news story.

The fire chief and J.P. hit it off that first day. He'd first asked for her credentials and found she didn't carry any except her press pass because she was just hired. Another reporter on site verified her employment so the fire chief agreed to talk to her.

So J. P. learned a lot about The Farm quickly. The chief demanded J.P. "Write this down. The Farm is new but no money was spared to make it the biggest, the best and the safest campus in the city. Big money went into all construction. The Farm's CEO Redding demanded the best and that's what he got. Money was no object."

Then almost with reverence, J.P. noted, the chief added, "The Farm is fully occupied now with the city's wealthiest and famous elders. This fire is probably the most excitement they'll have here for decades."

CHAPTER 3 – Jennifer Patricia Stein

God gives parents invisible clay to allow them to mold it into the personality for a newborn. Jennifer's parents made their only child a responsible, thoughtful and caring person, but also tried hard never to over indulge her. It worked. Always a quiet little girl, Jennifer on many occasions demonstrated courage and bravery from when the family's cat had to be put down to accompanying her parents when they took baskets of food to impoverished families. Her parents would ask Jennifer, after such benevolent visits, what she saw and how she felt. Jenny would give an accurate account first then often tearfully ask, "Why are so many so poor?" Jenny's parents explained the country suffered from a Great Depression so many were out of work.

One blistery Ohio winter morning little Jennifer received an unexpected shock. It scarred her psyche for life.

Holding on to the wobbly stair rail, Jennifer descended to the basement in the dark, as the only small naked light bulb with a long string attached was at the bottom of stairs. First up, the eight-year-old's job each winter morning in

1935 was to stir the furnace's sleeping coals back to life. It was the Great Depression and her household was lucky to even have coal.

Flipping on the switch, the child looked up to see a most horrible scene before her. She gasped. Her beloved uncle, who had moved in with them after he lost his own business, was dangling from a rope around his neck, lifeless. The act of desperation stunned the chiid but she did not scream. She could only stare. Then, realizing she must tell her parents who slept on the second floor, she tried to find the voice to tell them exactly what she'd discovered.

The words that spilled out were: "Uncle Jack hanging up."

That sent her parents rushing to the basement and into shock. Then realizing their little girl first saw what no child should see, they quickly rushed Jennifer upstairs to comfort her and try to explain the what and why of what she just saw. That trauma left Jennifer with an abhorrence of the word "suicide" and imprinted within her a strong desire to help others long before they sought that final solution.

As an adult Jennifer Patricia Stein made a career out of reporting on what she saw and others felt. That storyteller talent made J.P. an award winning journalist and later a successful author.

* * *

Jennifer did not grow up rich, but her parents were not poor either. She was an only child living during America's Great Depression. Her parents endured and later thrived in their mom and pop small restaurant. They split a 24-hour work shift.

Her mother described a daily scene for many customers: "Jennifer was born to write or become a great artist. So many nights when I work late, Jenny will busy herself while waiting to go home with me. She takes out the newspaper's cartoons and tries to copy them. She loves to draw. And she can remember and repeat accurately almost every word our customers tell her."

Waiting around for her mom to go home from the restaurant also introduced Jennifer to the seamy side of life and gave her a healthy dose of street smarts or knowing people for who or what they are.

Once regular late night customer "Jimmy the Tailor" and his entourage of young women came into the parents' restaurant after the bars closed at 2:30 a.m., hungry and with money to spend. They occupied almost every counter seat. Jennifer, then fourteen at the start of World War II filled in because restaurant help was scarce. That school night by her parents told her she'd have to replace the dishwasher who didn't show up for his shift then go on to school in the morning. It was an emergency.

Jenny sat on an orange crate below the counter, barely visible from the customers' eyes. She sang softly as she washed, trying to stay awake. Jimmy The Tailor (whom she found out much later tailored his girls to his customers' desires) came in dressed like the pimp he was, loud and often profane.

When he got up to pay his big bill, Jimmy, much shorter than any of his "girls", threw a five-dollar bill at Jennifer, saying loudly, "Here's to that lovely little lady dishwasher. Maybe someday she'll grow up to be as beautiful as my girls and join us."

Jennifer's father turned instant hero to her. He rushed down from the other end of the counter, grabbed the diminutive Jimmy, and called him a "god-damn pimp." Then he threw Jimmy out of the restaurant never to return.

Jenny later asked her Dad, "What's a pimp?"

Embarrassed, her father sidestepped the issue and said, "Forget it, Jenny. He's just a dirty scum bum."

Jennifer grew up a little that night learning people are good, bad and ugly.

Now J.P. wished her parents would have lived long enough to see her develop into a successful writer. Their support of her dreams had put her where she was today.

But thinking back Jennifer realized her parents would never have been able to retired to a place like The Farm. Hell, she thought, neither would she. Actually, her parents died long before they could retire anywhere.

The Farm's rich elder residents intrigued Jennifer. They could afford to live anywhere, so why did they choose The Farm's campus? Were they increasingly lonely and isolated as old age approached? Their answers might make great copy.

But J.P. had another growing concern. Would these wealthy residents open up to her and share their stories? Many were well over 65, but they ran with their own set. While J.P. was among the best of listeners, and had a talent for getting people to open up, would these Farm residents be willing to do so?

* * *

Actually Jenny's ex-husband, Ben Stein, could easily have afforded a place like The Farm for them had they stayed together into their old age. He came from wealth, even though he spent money almost faster than investments could earn interest. And in the early years of their twenty-year marriage, he taught J.P. to do the same. She didn't practice saving until it was almost too late.

What distanced Ben from Jenny more than anything else in their last years together was Ben's increasingly need for kinky sex. Try this, try that, he'd tell his wife, Jenny, who was ten years his junior.

Born in the conservative Mid-West of hard-working parents who didn't even mention the word sex to her (her classmates filled her in), J.P. found Ben's new brand of sex not just distasteful, but disgusting.

The ultimate breakup came when he asked her to engage in wife swapping. He'd met a couple through his work and apparently lusted or the wife. So he proposed to Jenny swapping wives for a while. "No big deal," he said.

It was a big deal to J.P. They were in a restaurant with that couple one night when the swap idea dropped. The couple thought it was a fun proposal. J.P. vetoed it by smashing her fist on the table so hard the glasses teetered. Then she got up and walked out.

Shortly after that it had been hard to tell her lovely teen-age daughter Trish that Jennifer was about to divorce Ben. Trish at 18 was tall like her father and as he was handsome she was beautiful. And she loved both parents.

After the divorce J.P. threw Trish another fastball. She announced they would move back to her hometown, Cincinnati, where J.P. would return to journalism and find a much-needed job as a reporter. Money for the move, plus buying two new cars and a condo near the University of Cincinnati campus, left J.P. nearly broke.

But there had been good years before. One good thing Ben Stein did for Jennifer late in their marriage was urged her to quit her reporter's job and turn entrepreneur to sell freelance articles to magazines. His inherited money and engineering jobs were enough to keep them comfortable in the high lifestyle he so loved.

Freelancing gave Jennifer a great resume to take with her to Cincinnati to impress the publisher of the Star-Times to hire her.

It had. Here she was on assignment ordered to write feature stories about the generation she found most fascinating—seniors. She felt compelled to show aging was a part of a fascinating cycle of life, not a dreaded disease.

Often she and Trish laughed about J.P.'s obsession to specialize in elder stories. Trish questioned her as to why write stories about aging? The youth culture was the big thing these days, Trish said. "You know Mom, don't trust anyone over 30," she teased.

J.P. laughed and gave her daughter her stock answer, "If you can't beat them, honey, join them. See my gray hairs?"

"Oh, Mom," Trish snickered, "you will never be old. You are too people-rich in stories."

J.P. smlled. "Smart kid."

CHAPTER 4 – WOLD

Miracles were part of WOLD's young history. A mother who listened daily to WOLD because it featured stories and music from her parents' era, brought in her 10-year-old son. He was obsessed with the World War II B-17 fighter planes and longed to meet in person a pilot who flew one. She asked if Carolyn would air her son's desire.

One such pilot heard the child's plea on WOLD and arranged to come in and meet the boy. Carolyn put them live on air and allowed the child to interview the pilot. It was a show repeated often. After that interview the boy left with a pocket full of souvenirs and a new hero.

Jennifer didn't leave the campus after she phoned in her sidebar story. She wanted a look at WOLD. So she stayed to talk to its manager Carolyn Armstrong.

They talked. Then suddenly Carolyn bolted out of her chair ran out and down to Studio One. J.P. remained seated, curious to be sure, but felt it best not to intrude in station business. Carolyn returned shortly.

"What happened?" Jennifer asked.

"Our volunteer broadcaster was reviewing a book on air. When he finished he said, 'It was the best damn book I've read in a decade.' "

"He said damn?"

"He did.

"So is that so terrible?"

"On radio here, yes it is. It could mean our license. I went to music, cut him off, and explained to our volunteer that we can't swear on the air. He walked out on me. Called me a hypocrite saying he sure heard me swear.

"Not on air, I told him."

Obviously upset she had to reprimand then lose one of her volunteer seniors who helped her run the station, Carolyn turned to J.P., saying, "Can we continue this interview later?"

J.P. nodded yes and stepped out, but stopped at the front desk to introduce herself to a stunning looking, mature volunteer receptionist busy filing her nails. Her bleached long blonde hair was up in a French twist. The black turtleneck sweater had to be cashmere and the only jewelry she wore was a single diamond necklace and stunning large engagement and wedding band. Her desk nameplate said Mary.

After introductions J.P. asked Mary if other volunteers at WOLD had a tough time adjusting to being on air. Most had no broadcasting experience. Nor did they apparently have a clue about rules of broadcasting in 1976 that Carolyn so meticulously laid out for them.

The receptionist recited the station's litany like a tour guide. "WOLD's mission is to enlighten, educate, and entertain seniors with music from their era, play re-runs of old radio classics, and live shows to enhance their retirement lifestyle."

"Nicely done. Do you do that often?"

"Only to nosy reporters," she responded with a big friendly grin. J. P. instantly liked her. She made note mentally to chat with Mary often as she sensed Mary might be a good resource to tap for Farm gossip.

While Jennifer sought out human-interest stories to enhance the image of aging, she had a lot of experience reporting on corruption in high places and unusual crime stories over two decades. She thought the later might not ever surface at The Farm, but were there any hint of one J.P the reporter would be there.

CHAPTER 5 – Sylvia Biggs

Sylvia was in early, as always. So when her phone rang it startled her. Annoyed to get a call so early when she needed this time to herself, she picked it up to hear a familiar male voice speak in a threatening tone.

"You know I know practically every move you make. Now I have the inside on what could be a big story for your new hire J.P. Stein. Don't screw it up by exposing me to her no matter what you hear. You know what I'm capable of. Understood?" Before Sylvia could reply, the caller hung up.

* * *

When Sylvia Biggs stood up to greet J.P. on her first full day on the job, the boss' right hand shot out. While disturbed by that early call, Sylvia was determined to ignore it and not share the veiled threat with anyone except perhaps the publisher, Tyson Cook. They were a couple now.

J.P. thought Sylvia was misplaced in the newsroom. She should be up on a big movie screen in theaters everywhere. She was that beautiful. About 30, blonde with a fashionable asymmetrical hairdo, short, cropped in back with a front piece provocatively hanging down over her right blue eye, she had long dark eyelashes other females would kill for.

Though small, perhaps five three, Sylvia seemed formidable enough to J.P. Sylvia wore a smartly tailored black suit with a light blue tee underneath, cut to reveal why, perhaps, she'd gotten so far so fast. She'd gone from reporter to editor in record time, J.P. learned through research and gossip.

Then Jennifer reprimanded herself for being so cynical. That's just rumors, she thought. She mentally chastised herself for jumping to conclusions, which was so unlike her. She knew it was not fair to assume that Sylvia might have spent some down time on Tyson Cook's famous white leather couch on the 20th floor just to crack through the glass ceiling barring women from joining the male executive suite. Sylvia's fast rise to management was probably just office envy.

Jennifer personally knew a lot of accomplished young women today who attained executive positions through merit, not employer lust.

J.P. exorcised her thoughts about her boss and her rush to judgment. Her own climb to success had been years in the making. It often was long, tough, full of potholes, insults and downright prejudice again female journalists. That was all due to entering a predominately male profession of journalism in 1949.

The sweat, scratching, shedding of silent tears piled up along side of J.P.'s push to get ahead. She bore unseen scars. She also knew while there were young women executives today who did skip the sweat and tears to opt for winning raises and promotions through personal favors, her own ascent over two decades was based on merit. Though tempted, early in her career J.P. vowed never to win a promotion any other way.

* * *

"Welcome back, J.P."

Jennifer took Sylvia Biggs' lovely manicured hand and offered her own best handshake to match Sylvia's firm one, which to J.P. was a surprise. No floppy hand shaker, or kiss-my-ring attitude either.

"Our publisher said you are just the right person for our chief feature writer new post that many wanted. Your performance under the most extraordinary of circumstances yesterday proved it. Let me explain our needs. We are unisex now, meaning men will read us as well as women. Our stories will vary from sex, sports, profiles, human interest, sex, health, nutrition, sex," she laughed, "Well, you get the idea. We'll try to Include everyone's tastes and interests to push readership. The goal for new readers is inclusion, not exclusion.

"Our publisher Ty Cook said we'd target men readers as well as women. We know from surveys what they like to read about. So I expect you personally to come up with great story ideas for this enlarged male-female audience of readers."

Sylvia's smile radiated her face as she described goals for her new department. So J.P. instantly relaxed. It was refreshing to hear a boss who loved her work as much as Sylvia did.

"By the way, thanks for going on that emergency stint yesterday at The Farm. We were covered, of course, but Andy and I both knew you were upstairs being hired. We thought that given your long experience in reporting on seniors, you'd benefit just being on that fancy campus during a real emergency to see how everyone reacted and get a lay of that land. Today we'll get to your employee paperwork, and discuss your salary and hours as well."

Whew, finally, J.P. thought.

On the job a second day and she had no idea of how much she'd make, what shift she'd have or what beat or beats would be assigned to her to cover. Her freelance stories in the past few years concentrated on ordinary seniors doing extraordinary things. One smart magazine editor told her, in order to launch her magazine freelance career, "If you want to survive, specialize." So J.P. chose to report on America's rapidly aging population. When Sylvia slipped her a salary figure on a piece of paper and pushed it toward her, it was all J.P. could do not to gasp. She doubled her last salary.

J.P. considered herself a great researcher, so she tried to impress her new boss by rattling off statistics she'd found about Star-

Times' circulation, its history and whatever else came to mind.

It didn't.

Along with Sylvia's beautiful eyes and body, there was a brain. "I did my homework on you, too, J. P. I was sorry to learn about your recent divorce, but I'm glad you decided to move back to Cincinnati and enroll your only child Trisha in UC. It's has a fine art school."

At first a little taken back about how much Sylvia had done in a background check to find out about her private life, J.P. took a deep breath, settled back and tried to relax.

Sylvia went on, first crushing out a cigarette much to J.P's delight. Herself an ex-smoker, it now not only annoyed her, it stung her eyes.

"I was a reporter, too, you know, before this promotion. And I always first checked out people I planned to interview, just like I'm sure you do."

For another hour they talked about J.P.'s job description, hours, benefits and where the lunchroom was.

Sylvia pointed out to J.P. that one of the tiny cubicles laughingly referred to offices would be hers, located at the far end of the newsroom. On top of each desk sat a state of the art new computer. The room was filed with smoke and full ashtrays, a drawback for J.P. now an ex-smoker.

Sylvia said J.P.'s assignment would be that of a "roving" feature writer—go anywhere, anytime, on assignment, to cover whoever or whatever she or management deemed important enough. Right now it was about life at The Farm as experienced by the rich and some of the famous there.

"Any questions?"

"Just one. Is this a new position or am I replacing someone?"

"New position, but much coveted by your peers. We know your many stories of late were on America's exploding senior population. You have a feel for them. That's good.

"We also know there are a lot of untold stories over at The Farm. A big number of the residents are retired from Fortune 500 companies. A former amateur tennis star and sharp businessman runs it. And its radio station WOLD has another celebrity who anchors a show. The Farm's star tenant Lana Koppler surprised all of Cincinnati when she moved there from her Indian Hill suburb mansion. We know its CEO Bob Redding created that penthouse just for her. He tore out walls, rewired, all to suit her taste, hoping, I guess, her wealthy friends would follow. What treasures she brought with her we can only imagine. So far we have not been privy to her inventory nor have any of us been invited to her famous soirees except Cook. And you know men don't reveal any of the juicy decorative details."

Lana's wealth was legendary, Sylvia said. Her reticence to do newspaper interviews also was well known to management. The fact J.P. filed a little story with direct quotes from Lana on her first try made points with Sylvia.

Jennifer had ended that little story sidebar which appeared on the front-page story with a Mark Twain quote to describe Lana's vitality.

"Age is strictly a case of mind over matter. If you don't mind, it doesn't matter." Even editor Andy Stokes liked that.

"Follow me." Sylvia got up and moving out of her office, allowing J.P. to tail behind. They moved down long double rows of eye-level cubicles where reporters were humped over computer screens to knock out stories. They came to J.P.'s tiny "office." At least her little half walls were empty of photos and calendars. Looking around at other reporters' walls showed everything from kids' photos to one that had a suggestive calendar pin-up celebrity. J.P. was sure her "office" would be the only one with no filled ashtray.

The computer sitting there on her desk frightened J.P. She had so little experience with them and no one here spoke up and volunteered to assist her. Most assumed she knew how to operate it.

The rest of the day went to routine, but the paperwork she'd encountered from personnel to join this staff was not. It seemed far too invasive of her privacy, which J.P. guarded well. She answered the question "race" with Caucasian. Religion? J.P. was tempted to flippantly respond, "God lives," because that question annoyed her. Instead she left it blank. She believed that what she believed was no one else's business.

Alone at last, J.P observed an envelope sitting on her desk. She opened it to reveal a desk key. She tossed it aside.

Then she sighed, looking around at the smoke-filled room in what appeared to be all young college grads turning out daily stories on their computers. She remembered when her daughter Trish laughingly told her today its youth's mantra was "Trust no one over 30." So re-inventing her middle-aged self in this youthful newsroom won't be easy, she thought.

After quick staff introductions, J. P. stared up at a split screen up on the computer monitor. On the left side of the black split screen was copy and on the other what looked like a lot of separated notes.

A sympathetic reporter in the next cubicle finally looked up, saw Jennifer staring at her monitor, and offered to quickly brief her on its operation. Her past stories were mostly written on typewriters, now dinosaurs. And that is just what she felt like today.

Up on the one side of the split screen a message there surprised her. Apparently earlier Sylvia sent her a note to be read now. On the screen's right side were notes for a story she must complete. Sylvia's note said, "Your little story on Lana added a nice touch to the fire story. Good job." J.P felt in her bones she was home.

* * *

While on The Farm's campus that first day Jennifer discovered sports fan CEO Bob Redding equipped his retirement community as though it was an elaborate fitness center, inside and out. Inside ere treadmills, free weights, machines to shape up arms and legs with personal trainers on the job. Large swimming pools were inside and out, with the indoor pool equipped to aid seniors with arthritic limbs.

Bob saw to it that there was a nine-hole golf course, even bowling lanes in the basement and four tennis courts.

No other retirement community in America pushed its seniors so lavishly into activity as did Bob Redding. While everything in and at The Farm was top of the line, rumors had it Bob personally hoarded his own money. And he insisted his department heads account to him for all their department needs and expenses.

Later Mary, the lovely, gossipy receptionist J.P. pumped at WOLD earlier, told J.P later that most other retirement homes supported a more sedentary lifestyle in 1976. Their CEOs thought Redding's new place would fail and he'd be pushed out soon. His emphasis on keeping seniors active was not widely accepted among other retirement community managements.

Those right now who most intrigued J.P at the Farm were WOLD's senior volunteers. She thought station manager Armstrong bold to hatch such a concept of using seniors as staff to make WOLD a unique radio station.

How did Carolyn put it to J.P.? "WOLD is a station of the seniors, by the seniors, for the seniors."

* * *

Perspiration replaced inspiration as J.P. wrote. The phone rang. It was Sylvia. "Go home early today, J.P. I'm sure we've overwhelmed you. Tomorrow hit the campus at The Farm and bring me some good stuff."

Relieved, J.P. gathered up her things. That surly young reporter Phyllis she'd been introduced to earlier and who J.P. was told by Sylvia that she covered the restaurant beat, stopped Jennifer's exit. Her facial scowl seemed permanent.

"Hey, J.P. It is funny that you use just initials. How come?"

"Long story."

"Cut to the short version. I'm curious."

"Later in my career when I started doing magazine stories free-lance, I used my full name Jennifer Patricia Stein. Many editors turned down my story proposals. Most were male who thought only their gender could write science, crime or medical stories. So I switched to using initials only and my stories sold. End of story."

That didn't satisfy Phyllis. She looked around, spotted J.P.'s handbag on top her desk.

"Hey, dummy, if you don't want to be a victim here, don't leave your purse out ever. Lock it up. That's why you've got the key all newbies get. We have someone in this building determined to relieve staffers of their purses."

"But I'm leaving now," J.P. explained, picking the purse up. "Tomorrow I'll remember to do that," J.P. said, trying to appease the young woman who lusted for her job and didn't get it.

J.P. edged toward the elevator. But before she got on it she thought she must make one stop to meet the chief librarian.

"Could I please take home your newspaper clip stories on WOLD, Jim Ticknor and Bob Redding to study? I'll bring them back tomorrow" she asked the librarian. He looked more like a kindly grandfather in his gray cardigan sweater and gray hair cropped short. But when he spoke his tongue was razor-edged.

"You'd better," he threatened. "Usually I don't allow clips to leave the building but Sylvia called in an okay if you were to ask for them."

My God, J.P. thought, two staff grumps within minutes of each other, young Phyllis and an older chief librarian. But she felt in her gut only one was trouble, Phyllis. Her "neighbor" reporter in the next cubicle, who'd come to J.P.'s aid earlier, told J.P. that many staffers applied for her title of chief feature writer, but none wanted it more than Phyllis. So, he said, speaking softly, "J.P., watch your back."

* * *

At home Jennifer enjoyed a pleasant dinner with Trish as cook, her daughter already an expert. Often J.P. teased her that if college didn't work out, Trish would make a great chef.

Growing up she spent almost as much time in her parents' large kitchen as she did in painting portraits first of family, then friends. From the time she was in kindergarten, Trish loved to cook and to draw. J.P. said the talents were in her genes. J.P. ignored her inherited talents but not Trish. She excelled in both.

At dinner J.P. hoped for real mom-daughter conversion about her new campus life, hoping Trish would collect many fond college memories as J.P. had.

Trish told her Mom she was excited to be on UC's large campus, meeting new friends, going to class. By starting out during a smaller summer session Trish felt she could more easily assimilate into college life. And though conversational this night, Trish still held back college details that J.P. was dying to hear. But as usual J.P. did not probe.

She and her daughter were on the best of terms even after the divorce, and J.P. wanted it kept that way. Now with Trish's entry into college, they would embark on another and different kind of relationship as one adult to another. She knew Trish would give her incurably curious mother more details when it was the right time.

Trish had become an adult, J.P. mused, overnight, it seemed. Thank God she didn't want to live on campus yet. J.P. was not ready to be an empty nester so soon after having to deal with being the only person in her bed.

After complimenting Trish on dinner, Jennifer moved into her sparsely furnished home office to study the Star-Times newspaper clips.

Trying to save moving money, Jennifer sold or gave away most of her furnishing from California and bought new to furnish the condo. With funds running low, she limited her office to a large file cabinet, a desk and chair, and a second hand tub chair next to a reading lamp. That would have to do for now.

J.P. studied the Star-Times newspaper clips. Many of them detailed Jim Ticknor's last TV announcer job that ended in scandal. A few of his sponsor's executives went to jail for cheating their investors in insurance scams.

But Jim, who also had invested with his sponsor, was absolved of any complicity in the fraud charges. He claimed rather to be one of the company's victims. The sponsoring Eagle Insurance Company went bankrupt shortly after the scandal and cheating many seniors out of annuity funds.

After giving many interviews to the press about the scandal, one of New York City's most prominent residents and TV super star Jim Ticknor announced his early retirement, fled New York to go to his hometown of Cincinnati. And to everyone's surprise Jim opted to move to The Farm's campus and into a plush Farm apartment. Why there? Bob Redding, Thickener's old friend and former business partner personally invited Jim to live at The Farm, even to picking out the expensive apartment where he had furnished for his nomadic friend.

Why there? J. P. struggled for an answer. It didn't make sense. A notorious womanizer and big spender, Ticknor enjoyed bedding celebrities half his age coast to coast as his prime avocation. Although 66, he didn't seem like the retiring kind. More even than bedding young women, he loved to flash and spend money. Stories of his extravagances were detailed in many news clips. Jennifer thought it strange for a living-in-the-fast lane Tricknor to retire to conservative Cincinnati. What was he promised?

Both Jennifer and Ticknor grew up Cincinnatians. Jim's lifestyle was that of a star in New York, used to flashbulbs and lots of press, which he loved. His ego, she observed in photos and stories about him, was almost as big as that famous and abundant white head of hair, so unusual in a man of his age.

But perhaps, J.P. reasoned, he took Redding's invitation to live at The Farm not for some promise of monetary gain but to allow a friend to settle into old age as a big fish in a little pond. It's better than no pond at all, J.P. thought.

At least at The Farm, unlike in New York, Jim would be among a lot of rich female widows who far out numbered the male population at The Farm, with more than 1500 residents. There he could be adored, supported and pampered again. But was that enough?

After reading stories on Jim, J.P. surmised that Ticknor's lavish New York to California expensive lifestyle couldn't be maintained here unless he had socked away a lot of retirement money to live on at millionaires' playground--The Farm. Unless, she thought, there was some secret promise of a big deal.

CHAPTER 6 – Carolyn Armstrong

Doom and gloom prevailed as Carolyn Armstrong pleaded with the Federal Communications Commission (FCC) for enough time to get WOLD's new radio tower inspected so WOLD could go on air for the first time.

But on inspection day it poured. The day before it had poured. All Carolyn needed was 15 minutes on inspection day to be rain free for the inspector to do his job. He couldn't come back for weeks.

Carolyn's sister, a nun, asked her religious community to pray for the rain to stop for those critical 15 minutes.

Just before the FCC inspector pulled up to the tower in his rented car, the rain stopped. The inspection was completed. As he got back into his car to leave, the clouds exploded, pouring rain everywhere.

Back at Carolyn's office the inspector said, "Amazing how the rains stopped for just those 15 exact minutes."

Carolyn smiled. She had a lot of little miracles happen at WOLD. It seemed a higher power was WOLD's best sponsor.

Station manager Carolyn Armstrong was more passionate about Radio WOLD FM than she'd ever been about any man. That is until last year when she allowed her current lover to move in with her. She lived in a rather large home for a single woman. It was in College Hill, left to her by her grandparents.

She told J.P. in girl talk off the record that her lover often invited her along on foreign business trips because she, like him, spoke several languages. Having Carolyn at his side as he walked into foreign businesses was unique. All men instantly admired this nearly six-foot tall lovely blonde woman who spoke their language. Tongues loosened and deals were made.

Owning a radio station was Carolyn's dream. All that money she'd inherited from her long lost wealthy father provided a windfall to buy. She'd made the inheritance grow through smart investments until that time would come and she could realize her dream to partner with someone to buy a local FM radio station license.

Her station's format would not play The Beatles, rock or country. No, she would insist that her station as the chief investor that it would play nostalgic music from the 1930-1949s. It would be the music of her grandfather's generation now the dominant population segment inAmerica. The station would be on air twenty four hours every day because Carolyn knew many seniors, like her grandparents, often didn't sleep well nights and loved to hear the music of their generation on radio.

WOLD would play Tommy Dorsey to Glen Miller to Artie Shaw. WOLD also would offer original educational programs on how to age successfully. Carolyn would also invite senior volunteers to write their own programs and air them.

Best of all, outside of a small professional staff, she'd invite many seniors to help run all aspects of the station and allow them the opportunity to lift the veil of invisibility society dropped over too many retired elders.

In her station's radio lobby Carolyn imagined a large plaque to honor her late grandparents who reared her into adulthood. They imbued in her a desire to help elders. They were her role models.

Carolyn's grandfather played a mean saxophone and taught music in Cincinnati pubic schools. Weekends his retired musicians' band played gigs, often for seniors' parties. Pa even taught her to jitterbug and play boogie woogie on the piano. Many times Carolyn treated Farm residents to a piano concert.

In college in the early 1950s, Carolyn wanted join her campus' all male ROTC unit. Tall, slim and athletic, she could have been the perfect poster child for the Army. But women were not allowed to join ROTC. So after graduation Carolyn joined the regular army with difficulty and was assigned to serve as a public information officer for the next ten years, rising in rank to captain.

"Early on in the service, I was raped," she told a surprised J.P. during their interview, "It went unreported. Oh, by the way, that's off the record," she instructed J.P.

"Of course," Jennifer answered, surprised that Carolyn would even ask.

"But why didn't you report the rape?" To J.P. rape was a criminal act and must be reported. She personally persuaded several women to do just that after she'd reported on criminal investigations.

Carolyn replied, "I did to my immediate commanding officer. He blew it off, giving me the line it happens sometimes. He viewed all the women under his command as freaks or sluts, showing them no respect. He hated the fact he had women soldiers at his base. Other service women told me they had reported incidents of rape to that particular commander to no avail. Those reports never reached the big base commander."

J. P. was stunned. How could Carolyn have left such a serious crime go unpunished? Personally she would never, ever, be able not to prosecute. Rape was a criminal act. Turn those criminals in. No exceptions J.P. felt.

"You would have had to be there at that time to understand," was Carolyn's answer. "It's a closed chapter. I'm not sure why I even told you. Continuing therapy perhaps?"

Carolyn had not only survived the Army, she thrived, winning many citations for her service radio shows and documentaries. Many of those awards adorned her office walls at WOLD.

Carolyn's wealthy father was a teen when he deserted her and her drug-addicted teen mom many years ago. She never heard a word from her dad growing up.

But after he died his personal attorney contacted Captain Armstrong to say she'd been left his considerable family fortune as his only child and heir.

Carolyn resigned her commission, determined to realize her lifelong dream to own a small FM radio station and target it toward senior entertainment.

Shortly after The Farm opened, Carolyn presented her plan for The Farm to house a small FM commercial radio station she would call WOLD, saying the last three call letters would identify it as a station for elders. She asked trustees at The Farm to partner in the ownership with her as principal investor. They bought into it because the risk was small and the potential for press exposure high. No retirement home in America had its own commercial FM radio station on its campus. It would be a first nationally. It might create a long waiting list to get into The Farm, insuring its longevity.

What troubled Carolyn, she confessed to J.P. now, after first saying "off the record, J.P.," was that she didn't have complete financial control over WOLD, which CEO Redding insisted on as his terms allow it to be on campus.

So all big donations to WOLD went directly to him. He never issued Carolyn an annual financial report, but always agreed readily to any and all of her budget requests. But she was told mostly they were breaking even. But if a WOLD big benefactor left WOLD because of some sort of disagreement, Bob would reprimand Carolyn for allowing good money to slip away. She didn't push the arrangement since she was iiving a dream and had a fortune of her own from her Dad's estate.

"So far we're solvent, I think," she said, toying with a cigarette she'd vowed never to use again, but kept it as a reminder of her strength not to smoke.

Because J.P. was so interested, Carolyn retold her how she presented to The Pleasant Hill Farm's trustees her WOLD plan for their campus.

"One trustee, a big cigar in his face which I abhor, came up to me before my presentation, pinched my butt and said, "Little gal, we've never allow women in our board room. You are to be the first. Be brief. We've real business to conduct."

"You didn't choke him or push his cigar down his throat?" J.P. laughed.

"No, instead I presented them with business facts they could not dispute. I had all the figures on WOLD's cost of doing business and how it could not only be the first retirement community to own a radio station, but it could eventually generate some real income from advertisers. It also would attract some high rollers to live at The Farm who might not otherwise consider it."

"That was a smart move," J.P. said with growing admiration.

"All my years in the Army exposed me to all kind of people, men and women. None scare me anymore. And no matter what male group you are making a presentation to, the bottom line is what really counts. I showed them our station could be monetarily healthy."

J. P saw Carolyn had strong business acumen but had to add, "Housing a small radio station on a retirement community campus using its residents as volunteer staffers on air and off is a revolutionary concept. They are for the most part amateurs. Was that concept hard to push?"

"Not really, at least I don't think so. You can't imagine how talented and inventive these seniors are. We could not keep the station open without them now."

"But will **WOLD** be able to thrive in this fierce city competition from all those other much larger FM stations? Sponsors like big numbers when it comes to listeners."

"We've rated well so far. Our sponsors like the fact too that their geriatric products are those used by our listening audience. Actually they fill a need to advertise with us. Our listeners are their buyers. Whether the products touted on air are eyeglasses or luxury cars, their commercials pitch to the choir."

"Had you ever thought of adding news to your programming? That's Ticknor's strength as a former NYC news anchor. It might add a lot more income," J.P. asked.

"No, I rejected it as I wanted to keep the station all entertainment and education.

However, the trustees and Bob Redding thought news might be a good idea. All other FM stations here have it. But those big boys push a mixed format of news, music and entertainment. Ours is purely music and senior programming. That makes us unique. News would delude that. Only a catastrophe would change my mind about allowing WOLD to do news."

CHAPTER 7 – Jim Ticknor

It was not unusual for TV news anchorman Jim Ticknor to party all night and report on air at his New York television station by mid-afternoon. Partying with women of the night was a lifestyle he savored.

One night when he was indulging in his passion for young women he stayed longer than usual. But by mid-morning he gathered up his clothes and snuck out, now cold sober.

Near time to go on air, two detectives showed up. His partner of the previous night was dead. Detectives escorted him downtown for interviews.

Yes, he had been drinking.

Yes, he knew the woman who is now dead.

No, he didn't kill her. When he left she was asleep, not dead.

His story held up, but not before headlines in the tabloids recounted all the details. Still, It didn't hurt his job status. Actually Ticknor may have even gained a larger TV audience. So bad boy Ticknor, as the tabloids labeled him from then on, got off easy again. Stories of broken hearts, dead bodies and large sums of money traveled with the bad boy wherever he landed. Yet women adored him.

Finally J. P. was able to set up a time to talk up close and personal with Jim Ticknor. After all, Sylvia wanted him to be a major piece of her many stories on The Farm because his name alone sold newspapers.

Before their interview she thought she'd visit with Mary the receptionist and listen in on the lobby speakers to one of Jim's shows before they actually talked.

Neither was there. It was early, yes but how could no one be there, since the door was unlocked? J.P. questioned herself and again checked her appointment book. She was right on. The station was open. But it also seemed deserted.

With her coffee in hand, J. P. slipped alone, she thought, into darkened large studio to sit quietly, sip coffee, and await her upcoming interview.

Noises in a dark alcove at far end of the room alerted her she was not alone. A woman's voice in a loud whisper said "Yes!" A male's grunt was audible.

Bewildered that she was not alone, J.P. peered more intently toward the end of the room where now she cold make out two figures, one male with abundant white hair and one female, who were having sex, oblivious to J.P.'s presence.

Jennifer made a quick retreat, almost spilling her coffee. She walked quickly down the long plush carpeted corridor to the receptionist's desk, sat down, and just waited for excuses that were about to happen.

None came.

Mary appeared first, a bit ruffled, but smiling and unapologetic at seeing J.P., even though it rather startled her.

"Well, you are early, J. P. Your interview with Jim is not for more than another hour or so."

"I know. I came in early to chat with you and to finish my coffee, then walk around a bit first."

Silence.

"So it was you who walked into the studio where we were?"

"Yes, it was. I'm sorry."

Mary again straightened her blouse, sat down, still smiling. "Well there's no use denying anything, is there? We thought we were alone."

J.P. responded carefully as Mary was a great news source and she didn't want that to change by offending her now. But she could not help but think, given this was The Farm, how inappropriate it was to have sex in the early morning inside a darkened studio of a radio station? And how daring.

"I'm sorry. I thought the studio was empty."

"Well, so did we. Jim and I are... well, just old friends. A lot of old biddies around here are jealous of me, I know, saying I'm celebrity mad and man happy. But I don't care. I helped Jim get settled here at The Farm when he recently moved in. He says I'm one of the loyal ones and I'd never discuss his...his... various interests with anyone. And I wouldn't. I like him. "

"I saw nothing. I had time to kill, so I thought I'd be invisible while I enjoyed my morning coffee, then go look around the retirement community before Jim and I talked."

"You know, J.P., in spite all the stories that say otherwise, sex is still alive and well in retirement communities. I ought to know."

"Entirely your business, Mary, and I'm delighted it is. Hey, I'm out of here for a little while. I'll be back when it's time to interview Jim, OK?"

Jennifer rushed out and back to the small café to order another coffee and kill some time. No one was in there yet and J.P. loved the place. Tables were wicker with matching chairs and on all three quarters of the walls were poster-sized engaging photos representing character traits in seniors. Each had a label such as bravery, courage, success, compassion. A large alcove in the back was set up to resemble a Parisian outside café complete, with tables for two. A large canopy covered the space. Each table had a red and white check tablecloth and a wine list. It was only open evenings.

Over the café's loud speakers J.P. listened as Jim's show went on air. He played music from the American Song Book of the 1930s and 1940s, such as "In The Mood" and "Green Eyes" then he'd break to describe in detail how wonderful his career had been, all the famous people he knew and paled around with, blah, blah, blah. J.P. thought it sounded like self-worship.

But, apparently J.P. had to admit, from what others told her, WOLD's listeners loved it, and him. And she had to agree that he was a good disc jockey and entertaining.

When his on-air hour was up, J. P. allowed Jim some time for a pit stop before their appointment.

Jim and Mary's tryst didn't surprise or shock J.P. She'd reported on high jinks most of her adult life, so it came as no surprise that sex remained a favorite pastime at any age.

Ticknor, she concluded, no matter how old he gets, was just being Ticknor. For a lifetime, regardless of where he was, he'd viewed all women as fair game. His exploits and conquests were legend in the tabloids. And, some women still loved him. They apparently embraced that bad boy syndrome, including Mary.

That alone didn't bother Jennifer, but his lack of respect for the female gender did. He barely tolerated the strong-minded station manager, Carolyn, even to suggesting once to the board, Carolyn heard, that a man might have been a better station manager choice.

And J.P. was sure he'd tried, and failed, to get Carolyn into some empty studio with his pants down, libido up. Had he tried, J.P. thought, knowing how tough Carolyn could be, he'd be singing soprano forever more.

When J.P. walked back into WOLD Jim was waiting for her.

"Why don't we go back into the big studio to talk?" he asked J.P.

To herself she thought, not on your life buster. Instead she suggested, "Let's sit down right here in the lobby so Mary can jump in when she can and help me interview you this time. Would that work?"

"It was you back there who barged in on us, wasn't it?"

"It was."

He smoothed his ample white hair, a gesture J.P. noted he did often, perhaps to assure himself he was camera ready.

"So?"

"So that was then. This is now. Let's talk why you suddenly retired and moved here recently to The Farm from your beloved New York City."

According to Jim, Bob Redding was his long time friend. His recent invite to Jim to retire and live at The Farm was to become WOLD's anchor and on air personality. Bob thought his fame would help beef up the station's listener base. And after all he was a senior.

"You are an investor in WOLD as well?"

Mary chimed in. "He doesn't have to be. He's a hit."

J.P. pursued. "You and Bob were business partners once, I understand."

"That was along time ago. We are of course longtime friends. But to answer your question, yes, I did put a little money into WOLD, I'm proud to say. It's going to be the best little FM station and most profitable one in America one day soon."

"It already is," Mary had to say.

Jim waved a hand at her as though to silence her and to signal that he was the interviewee, not her. It was obvious Mary adored him but the feeling was not mutual.

"But will you live here permanently?" J.P. asked.

"I plan to. Why do you ask that? Yes, I've been all over the world, lived many places including Europe. But it was just time to come home permanently."

"Did Bob Redding offer some big incentive to get you here, Jim?"

His bushy white eyebrows moved into a scowl. "What kind of questions is that? I'm helping out a friend being here, nothing more."

With that he struggled to get up out of the small tub chair, his six foot plus frame noticeably bulkier than in his prime TV broadcasting hero years in New York.

"We're finished here," came out firmly.

"Now Jim," Mary said, coming around the desk. "She's a reporter. She has to ask those questions, you know that. Sit down, I'll get you some coffee."

He sat. But he was annoyed with J. P's line of questioning. "Many have said in the tabloids when Bob Redding and I get together, bad things happen. I really resent that implication."

"I'm sorry, Jim. But you still have fans everywhere," J.P. threw in, hoping flattery will do what her straight questions wouldn't. "But you two have created headlines in the past. So The Farm seems the least likely place for you to settle down, unless there were some real incentives."

"You mean money? I am not broke as those asinine stories in the tabloids reported, and if that is what you imply."

"Of course not. You couldn't be and live here at The Farm, now could you?"

He smiled. "You're damn right, I couldn't. I'm unlike my friend Mary here, whose two deceased husbands' investments gave her the means to move here. I came here all on my own, thank you."

Mary looked hurt. J.P. found the remark ungallant and distasteful. But that was Jim Ticknor. She didn't have to like the guy to write about him.

Jim got up. "Why don't we take this interview into a studio later today or tomorrow at your best time?"

J.P. knew a dismissal when it happened. Jim Ticknor had secrets and her constant questioning might reveal some of them. But he wanted to regroup first, perhaps check in with Bob Redding before the next interview. His tongue was much looser than Redding.

"Of course, Jim. I could come back say around 2 p.m.? Would that be more convenient? I will bring a photographer for some pictures, too, OK?"

That pleased him. "A photographer? Oh, that's fine. Shall we say 2 p.m. then in Studio A?'

"That works just fine for me," J.P. said, shaking his hand and mentally washing it afterward.

* * *

"J.P., you have to understand Jim," Mary said to J. P. as she started to leave the station. "He's had his ups and downs financially and he is sensitive to that."

"Mary, his remark about your finances was out of line."

"I know, but you know it is true. I married wealthy men who all left me very well off. I've shared that information with Jim at times. Hell, we laugh about it. Just go easy on him when you talk next. He's a star here at WOLD. Our listeners love him."

J. P. assured her she'd "take it easy" on Jim's financial profile and left. Once outside the studio she quickly wrote in her notebook: "Jim Ticknor has money problems. He came to The Farm because Bob Redding gave him a reason to do so and it wasn't friendship. What are they up to?"

Back at the office to write some copy, J. P. felt somewhat drained. None of her prodding has turned out any really hot material. Perhaps The Farm wasn't a gold mine of feature stories after all and Sylvia needed to know that. Maybe it was time to wrap it up and seek a new assignment. The Farm seemed to have gone dry, story-wise.

* * *

She couldn't have been more wrong. Later back home J.P. received a puzzling phone call.

Trish as usual fixed a great dinner for both. Then J.P. went into her home office to work on a project, organize notes she'd gathered that day.

When the phone rang, J.P. almost let it go to voice message. She was tired. It was late and she felt disappointed that all her digging for hot story material about Ticknor, or the CEO at Pleasant Hill Farm produced zero as a peg for a lead story for the Star-Times.

But absently, she picked up the phone. A strange male voice in a low, almost whisper said, "J. P., you don't know me. And you won't. But I know you are doing a story on WOLD and James Ticknor, and Pleasant Hill Farm. I'll bet you didn't know that the Farm's CEO Redding and Ticknor were silent investors and partners at one time in a escort agency in California. And that it went broke, but not before they both got rich while their executives were later arrested for prostitution?"

"What? Who in the hell is this?" J.P. sputtered.

"I have some interesting stuff for your investigation, if you're interested. And knowledge of a big event about to take place there."

J.P. felt her blood rise. "Investigation? Who said anything about investigation? I'm a features reporter. I'm doing color articles and profiles. Besides, I don't take tips from anonymous callers. If you can't identify yourself, and prove it, hang up before I do."

Silence.

Then: "That's not going to happen. We may meet later, perhaps, but no names for now over the phone, only facts you can check out. I have documentation on a lot of Ticknor and Redding's past that should go public. And I have knowledge of something big that may be about to happen there. I can verify everything I say."

J.P. thought: *sure you can, you crackpot. Don't you think police over time checked them out? This is probably some angry husband of some woman Ticknor fooled around with who now wants to leak out stuff for revenge. Besides, how did this jerk get my unlisted and protected telephone number?*

He went on before she could respond to her gut feeling and hang up.

"You are doing a story on Ticknor and Redding, right? I know both of them. They could be dangerous. Take this seriously. I'll be in touch."

Then he hung up before she could. In her reliable gut J.P rationalized that something explosive was about to happen and this whisperer, as she deemed him and his whispered voice, knows about it, maybe is in on it. And he wants to spill his information right into her hungry story lap.

But another voice cautioned J.P. to ask herself: Why her?

CHAPTER 8 – Bob Redding

Being a Rhodes scholar, a tennis champion and successful businessman doesn't mean such a man can't have an out of control temper. Bob Redding knew at times his fury overcame his reason and he hurt people. Now his anger was directed toward one man, his millionaire poker-playing pal, who just threatened to expose Bob's latest intended crime.

Though Bob headed a nationally famous retirement community, he wanted a lot more out of life. He hoped to find it in Europe, and soon. But that's only if Wayne didn't mess things up.

Wayne Richardson, Cincinnati's former mayor, now the city's political kingpin maker, wasn't bluffing when he insisted Bob cut him in on whatever was planned at The Farm or he'd expose Bob and Ticknor's past. Wayne's network of spooks was extensive; Bob knew he must find a quick way to silence Wayne.

Preliminaries to execute "the plan" were over. They worked. It bought time. it must be executed now, quickly.

"Are you sure, Lana?"

"Damn it, Bob, I know when something is missing." Lana had called Bob in after the fire because she was alarmed. Damage was miniscule to Friday's kitchen but that wasn't the reason for this conversation.

"No one but you knew that Picasso hanging up there on my wall along with all those reproductions was real. Now it's gone. I've waited for it to be returned but I'm out of patience."

Bob shifted his weight, growing more irritated by the minute but knowing exactly what Lana was getting at.

"Are you accusing me, Lana? I don't know anything about art."

"Really. You spent all those early years in Europe as a Rhodes scholar and none was enjoying its art? I am sure you remember that when I moved in I mentioned, as workers hung my art collection, that one painting was the real thing. You asked me which one. I think I slipped and might have told you the Picasso. I am sure I did now.

"Or maybe at one of those good old boys' poker parties with Wayne Richardson here you threw out jokingly that Lana kept a famous painting in her apartment? Then some opportunist on campus later sneaked up here right after the fire and in all that confusion just took it? Come on, Bob."

Bob looked surprised at the mention of his poker pals.

"Oh, honey, I know all about those poker games. Were I invited to sit in, I could clean out your boys. And I know drinking is prevalent there, too, which always loosens tongues. Anyway, somehow, the word did get out about my painting. The rest of my real collection is safely under lock and key with my detective agency in charge. But in a moment of weakness I just had to have that one favorite painting put up on my wall because I missed it from when it hung in my house.

"My agency told me not to hang it here because too many strangers go in and out of this place for maintenance and security purposes. I ignored that advice because no one knew, except you, Bob, that this original was in my collection here. All assumed all of them were fake. And now it alone is missing after the fire. I gave it time to return, but now, Bob, hear me, I want it back."

Bob started to put his China teacup down on the marble coffee table, and then searched for something to place under it. He knew everything in Lana's apartment was antique and valuable. He'd personally supervised her move to The Farm and personally watched specialists install her secret wall safe behind a painting to make sure no one drilled into a pipe or something critical. He alone knew Lana's secrets but he also knew up until now she trusted him. It bought him time.

Lana pushed over a coaster to Bob for him to set down his saucer. She was mad. He knew it.

"How long have you known me, Lana?"

"Long enough to know you are the envy of every CEO who runs a retirement home. I can't imagine you jeopardizing all that for my painting, no matter how valuable. All right. Forget I mentioned it. I'm turning its theft over to the police. You've been a fine money manager, Bob, but lately there's been talk of missing items in residents' apartments and cottages. You're in charge and nothing's been done about solving them, so I hear. I know how much you hate the press, but they should be notified now, and the police, too. I heard you've told many residents to hold off until your security team completes its in-house investigation. But to me they are dragging their feet and so are you."

"You certainly do keep abreast of things, don't you?" The sarcastic tone was noticeable. "That's the advantage of being richer than the Pope. I have things investigated."

"Are you aware that many of those residents later found their items, and some owned up to senior moments?"

"Bob, I thought you knew I'm smarter than that. Those returns were planted my guys say to see if real thefts could be done. And honestly, do you want me to believe my gal Friday perhaps just took my painting down to dust or something, then I snatched it up, then forgot where?"

"Of course not. But most of those reported Farm thefts are back in their owners' hands. Remember my security team consists mostly of retired police officers. Top of the line."

"Even the new one, that blond muscle man?"

"Yes. Even him. He got laid off and I grabbed him up. He's formidable."

"I don't like him."

"I'm sorry Lana, but he's good. I'll just keep him out of your way."

"Do that. And if my painting doesn't show up very soon now, Bob, I'm giving you notice, my guys at my agency will call in the police."

"When? When will you report to police?"

"When my guys say so. I've held off. But not now. I'll do a couple more days, tops. Get it back." It was a warning.

Bob moved toward the door. "Don't show me out. I'll get on it, Lana, and get right back to you in a couple of days for sure. I know we'll solve this in-house. Your agency is good but so are my guys."

Yes, Lana thought, good at what?

Bob closed the door, hard.

Lana exhaled after taking a deep breath, creating then a deep sigh. She shook her head side to side, finally admitting to herself after much introspection over these last few days that this confrontation proved the demise of a very long friendship. And created an unexplained feeling of fear.

CHAPTER 9 – Volunteers

Miracles happened almost routinely at WOLD. True stories voluntarily retold on air touched many listeners' hearts, even changed lives.

An elderly woman one day popped into the studio to tell station manager Carolyn that her announced veterans' day special coming up must include a former Cincinnatian's story who had been a POW in Japan. He lived in California now. What he did with his life after the war renewed her faith in people.

The ex-pilot was invited by Carolyn to come tell his story of renewal to record as part of the veterans' day special. He flew in and recorded this:

"I was rescued from a POW camp in Japan near the end of the war. I was down to about 100 pounds from 220. Angry at their defeat, my captors stripped me of my clothes and threw me naked into a cage at their Zoo as an exhibit. They urged visitors to taunt me with sticks, me the skeleton American, to show that Americans were not supermen. They could be defeated."

But shortly after that, American sailors rescued all POWs and Japan surrendered.

Flash forward. That pilot in Post War America began a new lifetime career lecturing around America to talk to schoolchildren about the power of forgiveness. He saved his own life by forgiving his captors, including the Japanese pilot who shot down his plane. What's his message? He told teens for the next two decades: "Don't embrace hate: it kills your soul faster than bullets." Kids across America embraced him and his message of hope.

That veteran's special later won WOLD its first major broadcast award.

* * *

To J.P, Pleasant Hill was a fantasy farm. She felt a little guilty lately, though, on this assignment. The rich there laughed, loved and lusted. But that's not how most of America's seniors lived their lives in retirement.

For years J.P. reported on how hard most seniors worked to stretch their Social Security checks, often in heroic ways. Always there was more month than money for many. It troubled J. P that she might be giving a false impression to all readers that most retirees had it easy, when in reality just the opposite was true.

She consoled herself by comparing her reporting on The Farm's plush lifestyle and rich personalities to someone visiting a movie theater for a couple of hours to view a different lifestyle from their own. Moviegoers enjoyed the differences upon the screen that was so unlike their own everyday lives. Then they could go home to reality after being entertained.

Similarly stories J.P. wrote about The Farm's residents might entertain her readers, too.

So with a lighter heart J.P. went back to WOLD to greeted Mary at the receptionist's desk.

J.P. was amazed how really pretty Mary was, how full of life and pleasant. She forgave the rich volunteer her peccadilloes and obsession with the opposite sex, especially celebrities. J.P. was relieved older women like Mary still liked sex. So Mary liked men and they liked her. So what? Especially did Mary like Jim Ticknor. J.P. thought, so be it. Everyone's taste falters at times.

Mary was perfect for her job of greeting WOLD's guests and she provided Jennifer with a fountain of gossip and information not attainable anywhere else.

Every day at WOLD its house rules were challenged. Volunteers loved the station, served it faithfully, warts and all. But some pushed to the limits.

In this one day came an excited volunteer who sat down and silently went over her "script" in the lobby. Mary introduced her to J.P. The volunteer quickly excused herself saying she had to "rehearse."

J.P. was puzzled so Mary explained.

"She's a new volunteer and loaded. She doesn't live here," Mary said. "She asked Carolyn for a way to go on air as she had no interest in stuffing envelopes. But she also had no broadcast experience."

Mary said Carolyn thought of a way for this wealthy contributor to go on air. She'd use her in her new program she'd just created called "Up beat." She'd air thirty- second inspirationals daily, written mostly by the volunteers themselves. They would read them live on air or record for later.

Carolyn had this woman write and rewrite her too long script many times. The volunteer would bitterly complain to Mary that Carolyn was a too strict censor. Carolyn had cautioned the volunteer the message had to be brief. She'd heard the woman was somewhat of a religious fanatic so the station manager told the volunteer her message also must be inter denominational. And Carolyn insisted the volunteer read each new version to her.

Over and over Carolyn rejected her scripts as too long. So this day the volunteer popped in and surprised Carolyn by announcing, "Put me on. I'm ready."

"Let me see your script."

"Oh, it's just about the same as the others, only I trimmed it down to thirty seconds. I timed by my kitchen timer."

Carolyn happened to be on a tight schedule, so she smiled and agreed, "Let's go." The woman was so intent on doing this Carolyn waved to J.P. to hang on and they'd talk later.

Brevity was Carolyn's middle name. So if this wealthy contributor to WOLD was ready, compassionate Carolyn was also ready to give her a much-desired thirty seconds of airtime fame, live.

Into the studio the woman trotted, along with Carolyn, to introduce the station manager's new feature. The engineer signaled, "You're on."

Carolyn first. She nodded and began to explain WOLD'S new feature called, "Upbeat."

Carolyn then pointed to the woman, saying silently "go" with her mouth.

The elder nodded, cleared her throat, and with great brevity and emphasis said: "Go to church or go to hell."

Mary roared, listening with J.P. on lobby speakers.

Carolyn signaled go to music, escorted the volunteer out of the studio and into her office. She later emerged red-faced and vowed never to return.

Mary was loaded with such anecdotes about volunteers on air. J.P. promised to hear more at another time. She wanted to as she saw how upset Carolyn was to lose another big WOLD financial supporter.

CHAPTER 10 – The Whisperer

After Wayne Richardson's major heart attack, he gave up all hope of ever again running for pubic office. Instead, because of his extreme wealth, he'd make sure anyone else who did would have to come to him first if they wanted to win.

Rumors flew that he took his "other" women all over the city because in his long-time marriage to his college sweetheart, his wife told him bluntly their marriage would never end in divorce.

Through the years Wayne kept secret files on everyone who was someone or wanted to be. He had listeners inside and outside political offices, fire and police, who reported to him about friends and foes. He was a powerhouse and everyone knew it and tried never to cross him. Some said he knew where all the bodies were buried, literally and figuratively.

That same night J.P. received a second call from the man she called the "Whisperer."

"Yes, this is J. P."

The raspy male voice was back. But this time with a sense of urgency in his speech.

"Jennifer, I still want to remain anonymous. You will have to promise me that. I know your reputation to stand by your word. Legendary. I also know your beat is The Farm. Your boss Sylvia wants to know why Ticknor came to that campus. Right? I'll bet you'd give a lot to find out the real reason why, wouldn't you?"

"Excuse me. Who is this? A name, please, or I hang up."

"Don't. I know you're probably pissed I now have your private telephone number. Ask Phyllis how I got it. I also know you're always on the lookout for bigger stories than WOLD volunteers or Lana Turner's soirees."

"I'm listening."

"You know Bob Redding and Jim Ticknor are long time associates. Now I think they are about to mastermind a major heist."

"Are you insane? Listen, I don't take information from anonymous tips. Tell me who you are or I'm hanging up."

"Your loss. But I don't think you will. I know your reputation. A lot of years ago you wrote a magazine story about a friend of mine when he and I were in Congress. He's the one who got caught with his prostitute friend out on a drunken rampage in D.C. He wanted to marry her and he told me most of the media was out to kill him, except you. You gave him a fair story. So don't hang up.

"Oh, and by the way do tell Sylvia and Phyllis, the competitor for your job, that I said hi to them both. I'll be in touch very soon. You and I will meet. It's become urgent that we do so quickly. If we don't, people could get hurt, even me."

"Tell me who you...?"

He hung up.

J.P. immediately called Sylvia.

"Sorry to call you at home but a man just telephoned me on my private line for the second time, but this time suggesting a real crime is about to happen at The Farm. He won't give his name but when I threatened to hang up, he said his message was urgent. He also said to say hi to you and to Phyllis. Sylvia, enlighten me. I am totally at a loss."

A long pause.

Then, "J.P, this city is full of nuts who get their kicks thinking they are privy to inside information the press would die to have."

"This man seemed as though he knew you, and Phyllis, well."

Another pause.

"Describe his voice."

"Can't exactly. He kept it to a raspy whisper. I repeatedly asked him for his name. He refused."

"Try."

"OK. Very deep, almost broadcast strength. Firm and with authority."

"Oh, God!"

Silence.

"Sylvia? Do you think you know who it is?"

"I can't talk now. It's good that you made no commitment. Perhaps that's the end of it. But come into my office tomorrow before you hit the campus. We must talk."

CHAPTER 11 – Intrigue

Will you walk into my parlour?" said the Spider to the Fly, 'Tis the prettiest little parlour that ever you did spy; The way into my parlour is up a winding stair, And I've a many curious things to show when you are there." Oh no, no," said the little Fly, "to ask me is in vain, For who goes up your winding stair can ne'er come down again." The Spider and the Fly Poem by Mary Howitt

Even though her shift didn't start until eight, J.P. was at her desk at seven. She had to get a handle on last night's phone call before Sylvia called her into her office to talk.

But Sylvia came in right behind her, with two coffees in hand and motioned Jennifer to come to her office. They were alone.

"I knew you'd be in here early," Sylvia said, tossing her expensive handbag into her desk drawer, then locking it. J.P. observed that there really is a petty thief around stealing purses, not just another scare tactic dreamed up by Phyllis to spook J.P.

"Here, take this coffee. Sit. We have to talk."

She got up and closed her office door. Staff knew when it was closed, no one entered.

"I think I know who called you offering information on Jim Ticknor and Bob Redding's dealings. But what I don't understand is why he says it is urgent."

"Who is he and is he a threat to me or mine?"

"Wayne Richardson. You wouldn't know his name but once he was mayor of this city, a councilman, and congressman. These days a serious heart condition keeps him only in political back rooms as a kingmaker. No one runs for office in his party here without his backing. His money buys power."

She said this all in one breath.

"You know him from when you were a reporter?"

"I know him as my former lover."

J.P. dropped her pen. Embarrassed, she picked it up. She was speechless.

"He's a vindictive old man these days. He's still angry from when I broke up with him, but also angry with Ticknor and Redding, and who knows, maybe even mad at Lana. I don't know. They all have known each other in past dealings, so I've been told. But what I do know is if Jim and Bob crossed Wayne somehow it is payback time. Apparently they are on Wayne's hit list or maybe he is on theirs."

"Hit list?" What kind of drama was J.P. suddenly into as a player, not an observer? Jennifer didn't know what to ask next. She couldn't or wouldn't want to pry into her boss' private life but what kind of story was unfolding using J.P. as a whistle blower? And why did Wayne call J.P. to break whatever hot story he had?

Sylvia knew what J.P. was about to ask, beat her to it.

"He's still simmering over our breakup. But he's really more angry at Redding and Ticknor and from your phone call it appears he was cheated or left out of a deal so he's ready to even the score. You're an outsider. He figures you're not yet tainted by this paper's internal web. He hopes you will be the one to blow the whistle on whatever evidence he has."

"Could he really have solid evidence of some wrong doing?"

"That I can't answer. But I'd bet he does." She lit up again. The tears J.P. felt were real. Sylvia saw them.

"Sorry, didn't realize you were so allergic."

"I'm an ex-smoker, but now it does get to me, especially in close quarters. Smoke is about the only thing I tear up from these days."

Sylvia turned boss again. "My affair was not secret. We met openly for years. My staff knows of it. His marriage for years has been in name only; he couldn't get a divorce. Our critic Phyllis played handmaiden between Wayne and me, passing notes back and forth. Couldn't trust our computers. Then Tyson announced he wanted you, an outsider, as my chief feature writer. Phyllis was Wayne's candidate for your job and he blew up. Apparently Phyllis ran to

Wayne for comfort. So watch out. That's an unholy alliance.

"Now Wayne spends a lot of his time baby sitting an apartment for a friend at The Farm while his friend is out of the country. That's a big reason I assigned you to cover The Farm. Anywhere Wayne is, there's a possible story. He has that friend's apartment key, often stages poker games there for high stakes. They drink. He hears things."

J.P. was all reporter now and by instinct interested, but only in the facts. Not in the internal spider's web Wayne was spinning to catch...what? Whom? Why?

"So how does all of this play out on my beat? Shouldn't this suggestion of a possible criminal action go to the police reporters?"

"I honestly don't know. But I do know Wayne. If he is out to get someone, he will."

"But why tell me?"

"You are a well known national reporter, and you are a member of my staff. In his twisted mind, maybe giving you a big break might also bring me back to him. That will never happen, but he thinks like that. A favor begets a favor. He's counting on you not to reveal his identity for his big tip. Maybe someone has threatened him now, and that's why it's urgent. I don't know. But I'm sure your whisperer, as you called him, is Wayne Richardson. I not too long ago had an unidentified caller too only I knew who it was. Wayne wants Jim and Bob hung out to dry for some unknown reason."

"What could they have done? Any ideas?"

"None. But Wayne, Lana Koppler, and "the boys" as Lana calls Ticknor and Redding, once were all investors in Bob's corporation that bought out failing companies, fixed some, sold many for huge profits. Others they closed. Made lots of enemies. They also had lots of secret investors. Wayne often spoke of these deals when we were together, swearing me to secrecy.

"You were a reporter. How could you agree to that?"

Sylvia looked at her mature reporter straight in the eye. "I was a new young reporter then. He was a big time politician who impressed me. He also had a reputation of carrying out vendettas. So when he told me things as my lover I never tattled. Get it?"

Secretly J.R. was offended. She would not sit on a story to please anyone, even a rich and powerful lover. But then she remembered she and Sylvia were from different generations. J.P.'s strict code of honor wasn't as fashionable these days.

Sylvia went on to detail what she could safely disclose. "Jim Ticknor spends money like he owns a money tree, and always has. We know that. Bob hoards money, but always wants more. And Lana? Money for her is only a means to an end to give it away to help others, especially children. She is a great lady, a saint in that unholy alliance."

Jennifer couldn't absorb all she was hearing. What had she gotten herself into? Was she to be the fly in the Wayne spider's web? However, so far, nothing sounded threatening to her and hers.

But then Sylvia added: "No one crosses Wayne without being punished. But why what he's going to tell you is urgent troubles me. Wayne suffers from a serious heart condition. Perhaps he needs to exact his revenge quickly as his clock is ticking. Who knows? I personally think from what you have just told me the man has gone mental."

An edge of bitterness in her voice told Jennifer more than words.

"What do you want to me to do?"

"He trusts you, that's obvious. Let him play out his hand. Don't call him by name unless and until he tells you to. He wanted you to tell me he had called. Apparently that is part of his twisted plan. He knew you'd check all this out with me first. You are a good and loyal reporter. And I am your boss. But when he said to you to check with me and also tell Phyllis he said "hi" that was a warning to me to say out of his way and let him play out his hand."

"Will you?"

"No."

"But why did he specifically ask me to repeat to you, 'Say hi to Phyllis?' "

"It was Phyllis who gave him your private home phone number. That's for sure. He also knows that's against our newspaper's policy. Anyone who gives out a private number of any other members of our staff can be fired. So Wayne is reminding me through you his personal warning: do not to fire Phyllis.

Sylvia sighed deeply, suggesting to J.P. she was tired of all this intrigue. Then she added, "Wayne uses people. He knew I might fire her. So he's telling me to just reprimanded her without consequences. I know how he thinks. I knew Phyllis went right to him to recommend she get the chief feature writer new job, but our publisher Cook and I had other plans. Ty is not swayed by Richardson."

The way Sylvia said that J.P. sensed by her the determined tone that Sylvia and Ty were perhaps now involved more than professionally.

Sylvia again sighed then, added, "I swear some days Wayne hears everything I say or I do."

"Your apartment is bugged?"

"No, of course not. But Wayne is so rich and influential in this city very little goes on without him knowing about it. Spies are everywhere on his payroll. When we met I was a young reporter, ambitious and impressed by power. Today I am just disgusted."

J.P. had only one question left. "Am I or my daughter in any danger from Wayne?"

"Of course not. He's just impressed I found an ethical reporter. They are rare these days. He apparently plans to use you to get his revenge then reward you with a hot story."

"How do you want me to handle this?"

"If he calls you again, report to me immediately day or night. Do not let on you know his identity. Let him reveal that. We'll go from there. Let him play out his hand. Otherwise continue your excellent stories on The Farm. They are charming, especially those on Lana. You show her and many of those mature adults in an entirely new light. The readers love it."

Sylvia got up. That was J.P.'s cue to leave and try to make some sense out of this back at her desk. And to await the whisperer's next call, hopefully at any moment.

However she had company when she returned to her desk.

Phyllis was draped over a corner. "I see you're in the boss's office early. Bring her an apple?"

She made Jennifer twice as uncomfortable now that J.P. knows Phyllis was an instrumental part of this unfolding story. She now knew it was Phyllis who leaked J.P.'s phone number to Wayne and was Phyllis who expected and still wants J.P.'s job. And according to Sylvia, she will stop at nothing to get it.

It troubled J.P. hearing that her boss Sylvia was once Wayne's lover because that meant she had her own agenda in assigning newcomer J.P. to The Farm. If J.P. uncovered anything that would embarrass or even incriminate Wayne Richardson, Sylvia would be pleased. Or would she? Or would Sylvia order J.P. to bury a hot story once she got the facts because she knew her ex-lover's wrath usually ended in vengeance.

J.P. wasn't sure of anything, including her boss, Phyllis or Wayne Richardson. Even publisher Tyson Cook's involvement in Wayne' web troubled her. J.P. felt suddenly she was sitting on a time bomb.

J.P. asked herself: did Sylvia assigned J.P. to The Farm to let J.P. do all the under cover dirty work on Wayne, then have her suffer any repercussions from Wayne instead of her?

Jennifer now asked herself should she take all this intrigue up to publisher Tyson Cook on the 20th floor, spill her guts on what she did know then ask for some kind of immunity? Or has Richardson spun his rich and powerful web so far and wide that Cook, too, was caught up in it now?

CHAPTER 12 – A Visitor

Host to so many celebrities over the years, Lana had stories she could and could not tell. But she loved talking off the record to J.P because she was such a good listener and trustworthy.

One story that never was printed concerned Lana's family. She grew up with a physically abusive father and a beaten down farm mother. As drab as her own mother was, Lana had blossomed into a true beauty. Her own mother was jealous of her, third eldest of six and verbally abused her, too, and often. So 14-year-old Lana ran away.

She ran from the farm to Cincinnati and a job in a burlesque house where they presented live shows. Lying about her age, even though no one asked, she became a stripper at first. But her quick study and sharp mind, plus a great body, got her noticed not only by the show's manager who gave her starring roles, but by older men in the audience as well.

That led to her first marriage to a rich, old stage door johnnie who felt Lana made him young again. He died and Lana, savvy now to the wiles and ways of older men, was on her way up to great riches and power. One could say she earned her street smarts from on-the-job training.

J.P. loved being at the Farm and listening to Lana Koppler retell stories of her past.

Sitting in her lavish apartment recently, J.P. felt privileged. This woman was a saint to so many, spreading her good deeds everywhere without any notoriety unless necessary. But when a museum needed updating, Lana kicked off a campaign to make it happen with a big check in hand. She also sponsored a camp for handicapped and underprivileged children to attend cost free annually. Three major live theaters in town owed their renovations to her.

She offered J.P., as usual, a "hot toddy for the body." Lana should be 90 proof by now, Jennifer thought. But again J.P. refused a drink but this time explaining in detail why. She had an inherited allergy to alcohol.

"Honey, aren't you in the wrong profession? Journalists at my nightclubs could knock them down with the best of them."

Lana's drinking places included one club inherited from husband number one, a speakeasy during the Prohibition, where they sold illegal booze.

She described in detail what the place was like, complete with a muscled bouncer and a secret small door inside the front entrance door, opened each time there was a knock to admit only the privileged, just like in the movies.

Later on Lana opened two other legitimate nightclubs, courtesy of husband two and three. By that time, Lana said, they were called supper clubs. She played the gracious hostess to many top Broadway talent, movie stars and entertainers who came to town to appear in her club and later, by invitation, into her Indian Hill mansion. Some called these Lana's soirees, a tradition she carried over to The Farm.

J.P. looked at photos Lana produced of her last home. It reminded her of a European castle, all stone with many turrets, missing only a moat outside. She explained why no moat to J.P.

"Honey, I didn't need a moat. I had dogs, guard dogs. Mean dogs."

She'd told J.P her favorite stars who performed in her clubs included big timers such as Benny Goodman, Perry Como, Sophie Tucker, Bob Hope and one name J.P. didn't recognize. It was torch and blues singer Helen Morgan, popular in the late 1920s and 1930s, Lana said.

"Honey, when Helen draped herself up next to my grand piano, stroking that long chiffon scarf she wrapped around her little finger to sing, 'He's Just My Bill,'" we wept. She was that good. But she died young of cirrhosis of the liver. A real loss."

Listening to her talk of her youth, first as a teenage stripper and later a multi-millionaire after she buried three husbands, each wealthier than the previous one, plus gifts from a few generous "escorts," J.P. knew no feature story would do this grand dame justice. She was one of a kind.

Lana showed J.P. in another photo that was her study at the mansion.

"My God, Lana, that room is papered with photos, even on the ceiling."

"All autographed photos of America's favorite entertainers. I loved going in there. I knew I was immediately among friends. I had no family, so these talented people became my family."

"Why no children?" J.P asked.

"Honey, my plumbing wouldn't allow it. But I'm close enough to some of those camp kids they could be my own."

She was silent for a moment. Then Lana volunteered what amounted to a confession. Showing she can throw her weight around when necessary.

"I love to play bridge. I have two or more tables up here every week. Mary helps me host them. One of my regular players was losing her hearing. We hinted that she needed to be tested. She would not. So I faked a fire alarm going off. All the girls jumped up and ran out – they were in on it. Only the near deaf one remained at the table. We got out into the hall, gave my friend a little time to wonder and then returned.

"What the hell is wrong with you, Lana? Have you all gone crazy? Sit down here. I have a fantastic hand," her bridge fanatic complained, Lana said.

Lana said she told her, "Sandra, we faked that little scene pretending we heard a fire alarm just to show you if we really had one, and you were alone, you would not hear it.

That's dangerous. You have a problem. Now for all our sakes, damn it, get tested." She gave the woman a card. "Here's my favorite doctor. Go see him. It's on me."

The woman at first pouted. But she took Lana's card saying, "You all just did this because you knew I had a Grand Slam hand." She stormed out.

But she was back again later for Lana's bridge sessions with her new hearing aids. She warned the others, including Lana, not to gossip about her any more because now she could hear everything. That was her way of saying thank you to her friend.

"Sometimes, honey," Lana told J.P., "you just let things alone. But other times when people you like need a push but no one else will act, you personally have to set off dynamite under their chair to get them to help themselves."

* * *

Back in the office, J. P. couldn't wait for the "Whisperer" to call again. If this story was about to break, she needed him to call now and give her just the facts, some things she could check on and verify. He had not called. If the evidence he had was solid, she thought this might be a front-page story and her job security.

But she had to ask herself, why if his news was so urgent, wasn't her phone ringing?

Apparently it had at the office.

Phyllis showed up at her desk as usual mentally planning where to put the eviction notice for J.P. God help me, J.P. thought, I'd love to shoot Phyllis right on the spot. She is a viper.

J.P. asked herself over and over that perhaps a fast trip to the 20ᵗʰ floor might help resolve this mess she found herself in? But then how much did Publisher Tyson Cook already know?

Phyllis thrust several small message slips into J.P's face, a tease.

"See? Here's lots of phone calls for you, taken by me. No thanks needed."

"Why are you even answering my phone?"

"Oh, I hear it. And I'm close by. Otherwise you'd never know whether or not you'd missed an important call. You're out there in the field so much doing whatever it is you do over at The Farm that I just wanted to be of help back here on the home front."

"Or to monitor who is calling me?"

"Don't be edgy. Aren't you even a little curious about whoever is making all these calls?" she said, waving the small slips of paper back and forth in front of J.P.

Rather than put them down and move on, Phyllis perched herself on the corner of the desk, like a bird of prey spotting her kill.

J.P. snatched the slips from Phyllis' hand, slapped them down on the desktop and in her strongest voice ever almost shouted, "Get out. Get lost. I've work to do."

Phyllis didn't budge.

"Who is Paul?"

"What?" J.P. was startled. She grabbed up the slips where the name Paul was written on each with a telephone number and only, "Call me."

"The guy's persistent and it's a local call. So is he one of your seniors at The Farm with some hot tips or hot lips? Or is he from your secret past?"

"Phyllis, for the last time, get off my desk. I've got work to do. Now go, god damn it." The threatening sound of her own voice surprised even J.P.

Waving her middle finger up to J.P. as she retreated, Phyllis slinked back to her own desk while J.P. tried to catch her breath and calm down.

The only Paul that was stored in her memory bank went back a couple of decades ago to college days in California and to fellow journalism major Paul Casey, her "soul mate."

In 1945 Paul had returned to campus after World War II to start college all over again, this time in journalism. They instantly clicked and in four years up to graduation it was he who called them "soul mates," meaning one could almost finish a sentence started by the other. The only thing they never shared was a bed.

In college, J.P. insisted being allowed to cover male campus sports as the staff's only female. Males tried to freeze her out. Paul became her gladiator forever, always sensing when she was in trouble. This time both were assigned to attend and cover a college boxing tournament held downtown, not on campus.

College and city reporters crowded at ringside reserved for press, all male. As J.P. tried to pull out a seat, one reporter said bluntly, "No women allowed."

Paul, six four and all muscle, excused himself and walked over to each male reporter in the press box area, whispering something into the ear of each one of them. One reporter got up and offered J.P. his chair. Then the reporters suddenly made room for J.P.

Later Jennifer asked Paul. "Whatever did you say to them to let me sit in? Are you Irish mafia?"

Paul's blue eyes narrowed to look menacing. "Sure, I told them I was from Chicago." Then he laughed and said, "Forget it. They have."

Jennifer never found out what Paul said but she knew at least one male in the journalism department accepted her as an equal. Could these phone messages be from that same Paul? Had to be. But how? Why? He's off in Asia or somewhere as one of America's most famous foreign correspondents. She's a relocated divorced mother of one in mid-America trying to prove herself once again. Is this déjà vu?

On the slips in front of her she read and re-read, "Paul" and "Call me."

J.P. felt that same old spontaneous heat she experienced every time she heard Paul's name in college. She knew it had nothing to do with those sudden age-related hot flashes of late. This was old fever.

That college proposition of Paul's flashed into her memory bank. How did he say it? "How about the two of us running down to Mexico together after graduation tomorrow? We'll just leave all this behind. Have some fun then both of us get jobs as foreign correspondents to travel and work the world together?"

J.P. turned down her dear friend. She believed back then marriage came before cohabitation. Besides, she'd promised to marry Ben Stein. He'd promised to marry another shortly, too. So Paul Casey exited her life.

Now is he back? Why now?

CHAPTER 13 – Vengeance

Wayne Richardson debated whether to call Jennifer Stein from his friend's apartment at The Farm. Didn't want to leave any records of his call to trace. But he also knew if he were to catch Redding and Ticknor at something big they were planning, he'd have to act fast.

Last night's poker game tipped Wayne off. Both Jim and Bob seemed edgy, reflected in their betting.

"Something bothering you, Bob?" Wayne had asked.

"No, not really, Wayne. Why do you ask?"

"Your last raise. Reckless."

Bob pulled his cards close to his chest. "You think so? Call me."

Not only was Wayne an expert at poker, he "read" people faces and actions. Bob's reckless behavior all night signaled something was on his mind and it wasn't poker. Wayne wanted in.

"After this hand could I have a word with you and Jim in the den, please, gentlemen? The others here won't mind, would you?" He asked, pleasantly enough, knowing they would not complain. It was his game, his call. And he was Wayne Richardson.

Inside the apartment's den was a large round conference table of beautiful polished mahogany. On the walls were mementoes of the owner travels. There was even a photo of that resident and Wayne framed hanging on one wall. Nothing else personal was around, showing the owner wasn't there a lot. Europe was his business and his playground. The Farm was only used, apparently, as his R and R stop. But it had become Wayne's second home.

Wayne had a home, large and beautiful, inhabited by a wife who both feared and loved him. She refused him a divorce, saying basically he could come home whenever he wished. He'd used that estranged arrangement to his advantage, and often.

Wayne asked Jim and Bob to sit down in the den so he could look at each, face to face. He was a great reader of body language. "We've known each other a long time. I hear a famous painting belonging to Lana is missing. Not good. Lana's a good friend of mine. What do you know about that?" directing his question to Bob.

Silence. Stoic silence.

"I also know a famous art dealer in New York City, Jim, just had an anonymous long distance call to him asking if he'd be interested in purchasing a Picasso. Lana's Picasso."

Jim looked stunned. Bob looked very angry. He spoke first.

"Wayne, I know your spies are everywhere. Between you and Lana you'd both put the FBI to shame. But this is none of your damn business and it's far bigger than your fiefdom. So back off."

"I want in."

Bob got up and walked out.

Jim stayed seated. Confused now, he tried to pump Wayne a bit more.

"Where do you get your information from, Wayne? This time you are really off base. Lana's our friend."

"Am I off base? I don't think so. Why did Bob walk out? I also think, Jim, you're over your head in debt. Bob knows it. And that genius man is about to use you, again. Tell me some details and I'll see if I can help you. Bob's beyond help. Who has he hooked up with now? What's his big plan here and when does it go down?"

Jim clumsily knocked his chair over standing up. He smoothed his ample white hair in a gesture both born out of nervousness and vanity, the latter hoping perhaps at any moment a photographer might burst in and beg him for some shots.

Instead Jim patted Wayne's shoulder and said softly, "Too big even for you, Wayne," and left.

Wayne straightened up the chairs and sat at the big desk, toying with the idea of making a quick phone call to J.P., actually picked the phone up, then hung up, thinking it better to delay that for now. He wanted no records of calls.

It was evident to him tonight that Bob's new caper would not include him. Actually Wayne knew he had enough already to hang Bob, and perhaps even Jim. But he also knew with that exposure was some risk. His past was sordid enough, too, if all the facts were known, which they never will be. He had something detrimental on almost everyone.

Wayne thought now of his old friend, the congressman who had told Wayne years ago that J.P. Stein was the kind of reporter you should turn to if you wanted to break a big story but be kept out of it. He said J.P. had no agenda and stuck to the facts. She was not a mudslinger.

He sighed at that and remembered how hard he'd tried to dissuade his friend and fellow congressman to dump his prostitute girl friend before their affair's disclosure might cost him his long career in politics.

Lighting up a cigar, Wayne puffed and remembered J.P.'s story on his friend. All the news media was hounding the fallen congressman for interviews after he and his girlfriend were caught in a drunken ruckus in a D.C. nightclub and were thrown out and jailed. Everyone wanted the juicy details but his friend clammed up. He retreated to his Ohio lake vacation home and called J.P., inviting her to come to him to allow him to tell his side of the story for print.

She did, beautifully. Even Wayne saw his foolish friend in a better, or at least more sympathetic light.

Now, Wayne decided, the thing to do was have J.P. meet him here tomorrow in person and give her enough information so she could expose Bob for who he was and what he was going to do, and perhaps even save Lana some sorrow.

While it was hard for him to truly like and trust anyone, Lana Koppler came as close as anyone to being Wayne's friend. Bob had stolen her Picasso, he knew. What else did Bob plan to steal from Lana before he used those airline tickets purchased along with his renewed passport? Where was he going and how soon?

CHAPTER 14 – The Set Up

Regardless of how rich or influential one is during youth and middle age, or how big one's family becomes, come old age and new issues arise. One is loneliness. Some men and women try to regain lost youth by buying the love of the young. But it seldom lasts. What does last is the loyalty and love of one's same-age peers. They often become a senior's new family, sharing good and bad times together, with no agenda other than companionship until death do them part.

Jennifer enjoyed reliving Lana's past through her vast collection of scrapbooks. She allowed J.P. to take home as many as she liked.

J. P. selected a couple of scrapbooks from the 1920s and 1930s, periods in which America suffered through its Great Depression, right up to World War II in 1941.

Lana went through America's history of that period unscathed. Three millionaire husbands and some generous admirers left her one of America's richest women. She was a fast study, too. Not formally schooled, she with a quick mind learned on her own. She'd told J.P., "My education is in street smarts, honey. I have a master's degree in people. " And through her smart investments and picking smart people to surround her, her fortunes grew. She gave it away almost as fast as she received it.

At another of their recent afternoon toddy for the body "teas" which was anything but tea for Lana, she bragged that her recent ninetieth birthday party she threw on herself was "a blast."

She'd hired an entertainer from Las Vegas who sang so much like Frank Sinatra she forgave him for not being him. Everyone at The Farm came and wined, dined, danced, and had, she said, a glorious good time. That male entertainer insisted Lana dance with him.

He told her, "Lana, you're hot."

She told J.P. she replied, "I've cooled off a lot lately, honey."

Lana's last home, a 20-room mansion resembled a stone castle from the past, complete with turrets and filled with treasures. There were guard dogs in many photos.

J.P. asked her, "Why, Lana, did you want to downsize to this small penthouse here when you had such a beautiful Indian Hill home?"

"Honey, when you get to be my age practically everyone you ever loved or knew has died. With just Friday and me living in that big place it was too much, too quiet, too lonely. At The Farm people come and go all the time, even the damn security guys checking on me as though I'm an invalid."

Smiling, J. P. flipped through many scrapbook pages, admiring the beautiful young Lana, trying to image her as a teen, one of the real beauties of her time. When she was a stripper, J.P. imagined, the theater back alley was probably filled with stage door "johnnies" ready to escort her anywhere she wanted to go.

When the phone rang, J.P. jumped. It was after nine, and she'd longed to hear back from Paul. She'd called the number he left but no luck. What she didn't expect to hear was a raspy man's voice in a fake whisper say, "Want to talk?" Wayne Richardson had changed his mind and decided to call the reporter.

"Only if you tell me who you are."

"I will once we meet face to face and I am sure you are not being followed. Actually, when we do meet you'll probably know me. I'm well known in Cincinnati."

"I doubt that, I've been away from Cincinnati for over 20 years."

"J.P. I know all about you. That's why I picked only you to get this exclusive story. I can tell you why Jim moved to The Farm recently and why Bob's on his way out, quite literally."

"I'm listening."

"Please come alone to my friend's apartment on campus, 707 Trail Lane, tomorrow at 11 a.m. Bring your recorder. We haven't much time."

"I must know who you are first. I don't want to fall into a trap." She remembered Sylvia's warning not to say she knew his identify unless and until he told her.

"I'm sure by now you know my name after talking to your boss or you at least have an idea who I am. But no names over the phone. Tell no one I've called. Just come. We haven't much time."

Then again he hung up.

* * *

Jennifer knocked on the outside door of the security office early that next morning, which Lana told her never to do, as "They won't let you in from the outside." Jennifer held up her press pass and that big young security guard Lana disliked so open the door, all smiles.

"Miss Stein I presume?"

"You know my name?"

"My boss does. So I do. Please come in."

J.P. felt creepy and had no reason why she should.

"It's only 9 a.m. now, but at 11 a.m. I have an interview with a gentleman who often stays and baby-sits the apartment at 707 Trail Lane. I just wanted you to know I won't be breaking in or anything."

"We are aware who stays there, Miss Stein. What time did you say?"

"At 11 a.m. It's a press interview."

"And where can we reach you if there is a cancellation?"

"I'm heading over to WOLD first for a while."

"Very well. Thank you for stopping by."

"One thing, " J.P. added. "Are all apartments equipped with emergency chords in every room?"

"They are. Should you need anything, just pull it. We'll be there and fast." The way he said that troubled J.P. Had he some plan to listen in? Did security have hidden cameras somewhere?

"Why thank you. You've been most helpful."

He held the door for J. P, seeming anxious for her to leave.

CHAPTER 15 – No Show

When Wayne Richardson didn't show up J.P. Morgan felt somehow she was a failure. Had she once again trusted too much too soon? She knew Wayne Richardson was up to no good for some, but for her it could mean the best story of her career was breaking. On top of that the ghost of her past, Paul Casey, suddenly shows two decades later but doesn't return her calls. . Damn all men, she thought. Her mood was black, thinking lately too much of the good life suddenly seemed to be passing her by.

Jennifer knocked at first gently at the front door of 707 Trail Way. Then harder. It was 11 a.m. and she was always prompt. No answer. Then she noticed at the side a small button, obviously newly installed doorbell. She pushed. It rang. No response.

"Come on, Wayne Richardson, stop playing games. Open the damn door."

Jennifer was irritated and even a little scared. All that Sylvia revealed about Wayne made her wonder once again why this powerful man chose her to reveal his story when Sylvia herself might have been a better choice. Sure

Sylvia said she and Wayne were on the outs now but he knew Sylvia was first and foremost a crack reporter. If he had proof that could hang Bob and Jim, she'd be the most likely one to break the story.

Also a feeling of fear prevailed. J.P. knew Wayne's reputation. Sylvia told her Wayne was good to his friends and vicious to his enemies. Cross him, Sylvia had said, and you'd wish you hadn't.

Well now, it appears, Jennifer said to herself, she'd been stood up. Wayne is not answering the door. From his tone last night there was no way he'd forgotten this appointment. She wondered if the cleaning team who come in to all apartments as part of residents' housing package, might be in the vicinity and would let J.P. in the apartment? Immediately she rejected that idea. Security was so tight here you'd have to be the Queen Mother to gain entrance unannounced. If she said "police" to housekeeping, they'd probably say prove it.

Perhaps Wayne went out earlier and traffic delayed his return? She slumped down at a small bench near the apartment's door to wait. At 11:30 Jennifer struggled to get up, realizing forty-nine-year-olds don't cross their legs for that length of time. They ached. She'd take a brisk walk now and return at noon to see if perhaps Wayne had come back, would apologize for the delay, and they'd get down to business for a story that just might secure her longevity at the Star-Times.

When she returned again there was a "do not disturb" sign on the cottage doorknob.

That's strange, J.P. thought, this is not some hotel. No one does that here. But on the other hand, perhaps they do. After all, this is The Farm. The residents could and probably do call their own shots and management jumps. So if a resident (or in this case perpetual visitor Wayne Richardson) wanted maintenance not to come in for a while, it could happen, she supposed.

But her best gut instincts told her that's not the case. Something was wrong, out of place, but she didn't have a clue as to what it was or how to find out.

* * *

Returning to her main office, J.P. was stunned to see a much older, but even more handsome Paul Casey sitting at her desk reading a book. Hovering over him making small talk was Phyllis. It appeared to J.P. she'd taken out a lease on her office space, ready to move in.

"Oh, there you are, J.P. I told Paul not to wait at your desk as we never know when you'll be in since you are allowed to set your own hours and schedule. But he insisted."

The way she said that clued J.P. that Paul by telepathy was saying to her, "Watch out for this one." Their instant connection was back. He already sensed J.P. had problems and even after a more than twenty-year lapse, he was here, now ready to help. The gladiator returns, she thought.

CHAPTER 16 – Lover Come Back

When they were young coeds, Paul and Jennifer were almost inseparable. Both loved sports, people, and reporting. There was a time in their junior year when both thought it best they begin to date others as well. Jennifer met Ben and Paul met Patti. While there might be lust in their hearts, by this time both Jennifer and Paul had commitments to others. So they agreed they'd just be friends for life. Secretly, though, J.P. wanted to break that pact, but she didn't dare.

"I know it's late but have you had lunch yet? I'm here to take you any place you want to go so we can talk and catch up." Paul asked.

Standing up now before her the 50-ish Paul Casey made her think he could be next month's cover for some men's high-end magazine. He was trim, even a little thin. But to J.P. today he looked glorious.

"No, but I'm taking you to lunch instead, no argument, to a Cincinnati landmark, the Netherland Plaza. It's completely restored and as beautiful as it was in 1931 when it was built. Our restaurant columnist, yes, that would be the same Phyllis of forked tongue you just met minutes ago, who has raved about it."

* * *

"You come here often?" Paul said with an amused smile. He wasn't used to such high-end eateries while on duty, he said.

"Only to visit with a long lost friend. Paul, it's been forever. Tell me how you are how and how did you find me?'

"So many questions. First, remember, we were the stars of research in college. I could find you anywhere. I'm sure you could me. Second, I'm back in America at my boss' insistence to get this award in Columbus in a few days. I've followed your career over the years and I found you. I'm visiting a friend in Cincinnati so I'm here now with you. And yes, it has been too long since we last talked."

"Then you know I divorced in California recently and just moved back to my hometown with Trish?"

"I did. Sorry about your divorce. I went through that many years back."

"Oh, Paul, I'm so sorry. Do you have any kids?"

"They are young men now. One, imagine that, is a sports writer in San Francisco and the other is an attorney there. Their mother died a couple of years ago."

"Oh, Paul I'm so sorry."

"Thank you but that all was a long time ago. Tell me about The Farm. I've read some of your pieces."

"You have? How long have you been in Cincinnati and how long can you stay?"

"I'll be here visiting for a few more days then I'll drive a rented car to Columbus, get my award. I suspect soon there will be another foreign assignment. I'm kind of a nomad while in the Untied States. Europe is more my home. But I've acquired a lot of unused vacation time, too."

"I read your amazing stories out of Vietnam. That must have been hell. Is that what the award is for?"

Paul didn't answer for a moment, just nodding yes. Then, "Yes, certain parts of it were."

An obvious painful memory surfaced. J. P. changed the subject. As much as she didn't want it to end, she said, "Paul, I must go back to work now. Can we continue this over dinner tonight at home with my daughter Trish?"

"I'll pick you up."

"No, I have to return to The Farm. I'll give you driving directions now. Please come to our condo at 7. Trish is a great chef."

He took the directions. "Done. I'll see both of you at your place. See if tomorrow you can arrange for me to meet Lana. She's an amazing woman at 90 and a tower of strength to others, it appears from your stories. A couple I knew and befriended in Vietnam had a grandmother about her age. She too was an amazing woman. Lana's strength came out in your stories on her."

Pleased he'd read her stories of late as she had his over the years from Asia to Africa to

Europe, they hugged and went their separate ways. Until tonight, then, she thought. Again heat flushed in her, apparently was attributed to his nearness, not her middle-age biological time clock.

CHAPTER 17 – Three To Get Ready

"Do you think we'll ever be lovers, Jenny?" Paul asked. They'd returned from seeing a movie on the eve of their college graduation. "I know we've both committed to other people but something is not right. Not right at all." Paul took Jenny's hand preventing her from opening the car door. We belong together."

"Paul, we're been through this. We are great friends but I promised to marry Ben and you will marry soon, too."

"I'm not talking marriage. Let's just run way. We both want the same thing, to be reporters. We should just do it together."

All Jenny's instincts told her to get out of Paul's car now, wave goodbye, and mean it.

She did.

Trish, alerted by a phone call that her mom's "Paul" was coming to dinner, outdid herself with the meal's cuisine. Accidentally, while packing up to move to Cincinnati, Trish found several of her mother's scrapbooks containing Paul Casey's stories cut out and saved from newspapers around the world. She suspected he was very special to her Mom at one time.

J.P. was so proud of her daughter. She managed a fast but sumptuous dinner on short notice and had the tact to excuse herself shortly after dinner so Paul and she could move to their living room for after dinner refreshments and conversation.

"Brandy, Paul?

"I see you don't still imbibe," he remembered, taking a glass from J.P.

"The problem remains. Alcohol and I are enemies."

Never, Jennifer admitted to herself now, had any man made her feel—what? --feverish as Paul did and that included her ex, Ben Stein. That internal "heat" she felt anytime she was near Paul so long ago, now, to her embarrassment, never left.

"How were those last days in Vietnam?"

"You read about them, I'm sure. They were among my most terrible war memories."

"And that family you wrote about that you tried to evacuate on one of the last helicopter lifts out?"

"Didn't happen. The couple, their two children and the kids' great grandma showed up too late. We were in the air. Left them looking up, us staring down at them on the ground." His sigh was long, the following silence prolonged.

J.P. put her hand on his arm. "Paul, I'm so sorry. You did what you had to do, I'm sure they understood."

"Until I get them safely here to the United States I won't rest." Spontaneously Jennifer hugged him.

He got up, changing the subject. "Nice place you have here. Your daughter is terrific."

Jennifer lightened up, too. "Trish is about six inches taller than me. That she got from her father. But I claim her street smarts and her gift for liking people –that comes from me."

Paul's hearty laugh was good to hear. It was late when he left, but not before J.P. promising early in the morning to contact Lana to see if they might come to her place before Paul had to leave. He wanted to meet the grand dame. Although on the exploding end of a hot story, she could, for Paul's sake, put it off for an hour or so early tomorrow. They say in crises one's entire life can swirl before your mental eyes. Right now J.P.'s past merged into today's reunion with Paul to afford her new sweet memories, and she loved it.

* * *

"Let's don't take the elevator up to five," Paul suggested as J. P. led him into Lana's building. "I try to stay fit by avoiding elevators."

At the top, J.P. realized she must start doing stairs more often. He was way ahead of her.

Lana hugged Paul as though he were an old friend. She winked past his broad shoulder to J.P., as though to say, "Honey, you did good."

Friday provided real tea for them and mid-morning treats but J.P. noticed Paul ate just enough so as not to offend his hostess.

"I knew a Vietnam grandmother who loved children as much as J.P.'s stories tell me you do, Lana."

"She's a persistent reporter, Paul, dragging stuff out of me I hadn't intended to tell anyone. A penalty of longevity, today I have no close family alive except those kids and my dear friend Friday. But watch those distant relatives come out of the woodwork at my wake."

She laughed hard enough to produce that deep persistent cough.

"Did J.P. tell you about Wayne Richardson's attempt to dump all his dirty linen into her lap, then never showed up to reveal his information?"

"No, she didn't." He smiled at J.P., his eyes saying what's this? Will you tell me later? He looked concerned at J. P., who shrugged her shoulders, pointing to her watch. After all this was her story to file. So Lana did not fill Paul in on details of the mysterious hot tip Wayne Richardson had promised Jennifer but never delivered.

They stayed longer than J.P. should have but then Paul said he had to go, promising Lana some real time to get better acquainted after his award ceremony.

But both Paul and J.P. were jarred by what they viewed as they stepped outside Lana's building to go their separate ways. Cars, ambulances, TV cameras and police were everywhere. She saw the Star-Times police reporter approaching her. She threw Paul a kiss and with her mouth silently said, "Call me," and ran off.

"What's going on, Steve?" she asked the Star-Times police reporter.

"They found a body in one of apartments."

"Which one?" she pleaded to herself, please not 707.

"On Trails' Way. It's 707."

J.P ran to the location, flashed her press pass, and gained access inside to see police interviewing a disturbed and uncooperative Bob Redding. His dislike of being interviewed first by police and now a reporter showed. On the floor lay. she assumed. Wayne Richardson. She knew it had to be him in that elegant smoking jacket, showing a bit of blood on his forehead, and a face badly bruised.

She moved over to a plainclothes detective. "How did he die?"

Irritated, he said, "Your guy over there already questioned me. Ask him."

She didn't move.

The detective realized she wasn't going anywhere so he elaborated a bit. "Wayne probably had a heart attack, which the coroner soon will confirm. Everyone knows about Wayne's heart problems. A natural death."

That shook up J.P. "What are you saying?"

"Everyone knows Wayne quit politics after his heart attack. You can't live or work in this city without knowing or hearing about Wayne, his tactics and his women. He was so rich only The Farm's Lana Koppler tops him."

"The room's kind of a mess, isn't it? Did all that occur just from his fall?" J.P. asked.

"Looks that way, probably tried to catch himself."

"Who reported it?"

"A Farm housekeeper found him, told Bob Redding, and he called it in."

J.P. heard enough. She rushed out and down to WOLD and to Carolyn, who already was live on air trying to soothe campus residents not to fear the sirens and traffic outside on Bob's pristine grounds. She was saying into the microphone, "A visitor who was a friend of a Farm resident suffered a fatal heart attack in his apartment this morning and died. His name is Wayne Richardson, former Congressman and mayor. The police will be winding up here shortly. But we'll try to bring for you interviews with Mr. Richardson's friends, WOLD's anchor Jim Ticknor and CEO Bob Redding. More details shortly. For now let's go back to the music you love to hear at WOLD FM."

For a station that never did news, Carolyn sounded great live on air doing just that, J.P. thought.

Mary was in the lobby, softly crying.

"You knew Wayne?" J.P. asked.

"Didn't everyone?" she sobbed. "He's a bastard to most, but not to me. My late husband did business with Wayne for years. Wayne had a bad heart."

J.P. stayed to comfort her a bit and also to listen to see if in sorrow Mary revealed anything else about Wayne other than his heart that might explain his sudden death. Why J.P. felt so anxious she didn't know, but Wayne's death after not keeping their "urgent" appointment to reveal criminal intent of some kind by Bob Redding and Jim Ticknor plain scared her.

CHAPTER 18 – A Puzzle

Routine describes housekeepers' duties at The Farm. Each had specific apartments and cottages to clean on specific days. Most residents are home when housekeepers come. So when one of Annie's apartments had a "Do Not Disturb" sign on the front door it was no longer routine.

At home J.P. sorted out her notes, her filed stories, and her fears.

Her boss was part of the hot story unfolding at The Farm. Some of the main players were, if not yet criminals, might soon become ones. Her beloved Lana was involved someway, somehow, in what was about to explode at The Farm, according to the late Wayne Richardson. And did Wayne die a natural death, or not?

Police reporter Stokes told J. P. the black housekeeper Annie who found Wayne's body first saw a "Do Not Disturb" sign on the door at 707 and thought it odd, since the owner was away. She called Bob Redding. No answer. Rather than double back later, Annie decided to use the passkey and just go in. She screamed. Lying on the floor was Wayne's body. She dropped her supplies and ran for Redding's office to get help.

J.P. wondered why Annie didn't call campus security or police. Carolyn cleared that matter up. Annie feared any city police contact from that unwritten rule in the ghetto not to trust police. She didn't' quite trust campus security either she told Carolyn later.

A gentle knock on Jennifer's home office door startled J.P. It was Trish.

"Mom, is everything all right? You've been in here a long time and I'm worried about you."

"Don't be. But come in Trish and sit down."

Her tone scared Trish. This was a mother who sounded different, even somber.

"The story I'm covering at The Farm has taken a criminal turn, I fear. A man died there today of reported natural causes. But I think maybe not. Police said it was a natural death. But the dead man was the same man who was about to tell J.P. details that would have exposed Jim Ticknor and CEO Bob Redding as frauds or worse.

"That man who died, Wayne Richardson, was powerful in this city, rich and vindictive. Who knows who might have wished him dead? But everyone assumes he died of a heart attack and that's official."

Trish asked, "And you don't?"

"Not sure. I'm sitting here going over all my past stories and notes trying to put all the pieces of a puzzle together."

"Is your friend Lana involved in anyway?"

"Asked like a true reporter," J. P. said, now smiling as she took her daughter's hand. "I honestly don't know. I do know all the principals at The Farm and in my stories have a past together."

"You always report what you know factually. Why not do just that?"

"I will, but it is just not that simple. And I'm not sure what is fact, revenge or criminal. These aren't the kind of stories I usually write about. I'm a little out of my league. Why don't you go on to bed? I'm going to sit here awhile to do some sorting out."

Trish kissed her Mother's brow and left.

In her short time on her assignment at The Farm, J.P. had more questions than answers. Her prime concern right now: was Trish or she in any danger from events erupting at the Farm? Was Wayne's death natural or did someone push him around to cause a heart attack? Were those facial bruises from his fall, or administered before the fall?

And why would anyone try to harm Wayne, J.P. pondered. Could it be to gain information, silence him or give someone else enough time to execute a plan? And most disturbing, was her visit to security prior to her appointment with Wayne a factor in his sudden death?

Security, J.P. reasoned, knew of her appointment because she told the blonde giant guard the time of her Wayne appointment just for her own safety's sake. So was she responsible for Wayne's death? Did she unknowingly send an assassin to Wayne's apartment before he could talk?

That's when J.P. noticed some of her old scrapbooks on top of her big desk. She smiled thinking Trish was at it again going through a few as she had in the past, perhaps this time with Trish trying to rediscover her mom's past through clippings revealing old memories.

J.P. loved those old scrapbooks because she felt by looking in them from time to time it gave her a chance to be like Alice In Wonderland, viewing her own past through a looking glass.

It seemed now so long ago when the thought of being a reporter was exciting, romantic. But at age eight her career dream momentarily burst.

J.P. took out a scrapbook that showed a photo of herself in her Mom's kitchen using a toy typewriter to publish her first edition of "The Paul Street Weekly." Jennifer's Dad took that photo of her and the first and last copy of her first publication.

In that childhood newsletter Jennifer detailed the next-door neighbor's teen who threw a wild party while his parents vacationed. When the parents returned and saw Jennifer's copy of The Paul Street Weekly's they threatened Jennifer's parents with a lawsuit if it didn't cease publication immediately. So all the remaining copies of The Paul Street Weekly were burned. Jennifer's toy typewriter went silent.

Now that memory brought a laugh from J. P. A much needed laugh. Even at the tender age of eight she was always looked for a great story, and to hell with the consequences. Her entire life up to this point, it seemed, was never give up on a story.

But today's event was far more complicated. Revealing what she knew or thought she knew may be dangerous. Had she already put her family and friends in danger? And if so, who was her enemy?

So far she'd covered so many aspects in the lives of those who lived or worked at The Farm. They deserved the truth. Jennifer had matured since she'd reported on The Farm's residents. She viewed reporting on aging as an opportunity to celebrate life, not fear it. Perhaps some of that senior optimism might rub off on her.

Such as Annie's story of hope told on WOLD with Carolyn as her interviewer. Annie told J.P. that day she didn't know anything more about Richardson's death other than it was she who found him dead. She did tell J.P. that "Do Not Disturb" sign was strange and that she'd earlier spotted an unidentified man putting it there. That's why she went in.

Annie said on air police and government people were always bad news. "My single granddaughter had two babies to support but she didn't. Any money she got her hands on went for drugs. Social Services intervened to give Annie an ultimatum: You take in the two great grandchildren or they go into foster home care system.

"I loved my grandbabies, but I was barely surviving on my meager SSI checks. How could I afford to care for two more at my age? I asked if government would give me child support? But she said no, only foster parents got subsidies. Right then I said I'll take the babies, anyway. No foster care for me and mine. God help us."

Carolyn knew her WOLD audience was glued to their radios listening to this profile in courage with a surprise ending.

Desperate for money, Annie had an inspiration. Known by neighbors as a fabulous baker, she asked herself why not sell baked goods? She went door-to-door and street-to-street corner to offer baked goods for cash.

It worked. Demand grew. She opened a tiny weekend storefront bakery with help from that empathetic social worker. Then she was able to go to part-time housekeeping at The Farm to supplement her come. However, the day she found Wayne Richardson dead shocked her. She quit.

Lana heard that interview, too. An immediate phone call to Carolyn gave impoverished Annie a large cash gift for her and the two grandbabies.

J.P. did reach Annie to question her further.

"Did you notice anything strange in that apartment where you found Mr. Richardson?"

"No, just the mess. There were papers on the floor, a small table was overturned and a lamp was on the floor."

"Wasn't that unusual? Did you touch anything?"

"No I didn't. I was so frightened I just ran off out of there."

CHAPTER 19 – Bookkeeping

Carolyn knew right after WOLD went on air it had been a mistake to allow Bob to take charge of all of WOLD's financials. But her dream of owning a small radio FM station for seniors was so all consuming she agreed to his terms, thinking that once WOLD was established, she, as its prime investor, would insist upon change. After all, she reasoned, it was Bob Redding who helped her win over The Farm's trustees, many of whom were cool to putting a radio station on campus. Redding had told trustees in a few years WOLD would make money for The Farm as well as for Carolyn. Bob then vacating several rooms to accommodate the station, transforming that space into a top of the line FM radio station, complete with offices for staff, a huge lounge and equipped volunteer room, and three large state-of-the-art studios, mostly with Carolyn's money. Because she was so well fixed, Bob knew she'd not press him for particulars about the large donations coming in and income from commercials for the short term, which was all the time he needed to execute "the plan."

J.P. wondered how levelheaded Carolyn could agree to Bob Redding 's edict that he alone would keep the books and never reveal to her, a major partner, her profit and loss. "Simple, he said to Carolyn and reported back to friend J.R., "WOLD is just a hobby for you, rich lady. So I'm sure you'll let me monitor its finances for a while because it is such a radical idea. Of course we will cover all expenses above what you invested to get the station on solid ground."

Carolyn had called Jennifer in to her office for talk. The station manager said she'd decided now to change all that and demand an outside audit soon as she was sure WOLD wouldn't be hurt in the process. "Can I talk off the record on that subject?"

J.P nodded yes.

"I think now that the board of trustees see one set of books on WOLD and Bob keeps a second secret set. How do I know this? Jim slipped one day and laughed about, which he called, Bob's genius for creative bookkeeping."

J.P. didn't know how far to push for more details without involving Carolyn. Were she to confront Bob about this, she might also have a sudden accident, Jennifer thought.

So guardedly she asked, "That sounds illegal to me, Carolyn. Do you think he does that to avoid taxes?"

"I'm not sure it is even true. Jim, as you know now, likes to leak inflated information just to get a reaction. He also enlarges on the truth, a lot."

Now we are on the same page, J.P. thought. Carolyn knows things aren't quite kosher here, as Wayne Richardson knew, but Carolyn doesn't know how to confront her partners.

"Carolyn, I tell you this for your own safety. Something is going on here at The Farm that is frightening. I don't think Wayne Richardson, who knew something about Bob's accounts, died of natural causes, but I can't prove it.

"I think someone got to him before my appointment. Someone roughed him up and caused his sudden heart attack. It was deliberate. He had bruises on his face that seemed to me more than from a straight down fall. But the coroner ruled it death by natural causes. So until we clear this all up, please don't pursue your interest in seeking the audit. Not just yet."

Carolyn toyed again with an unlit cigarette, her prop to remind her not to smoke, and then asked, "How are you going to prove your theory?"

"I have sources alerting me. Wayne would have solved the mystery. He's gone. Now I'm banking on Lana."

"Oh, J.P., be careful. There are so many big, powerful interests here it boggles your mind. I just want to protect my WOLD resources so we can grow. I've a big investment here, too. And Jim's show has been a big asset. We've more listeners than ever so I hope he's not involved in anything with Bob."

J.P. didn't want to answer that. Instead she got up, told Carolyn she'd stay in touch, and left, reminding her for now not to disclose their conversation.

But before she could leave WOLD Mary grabbed her arm and said, "J.P., can we talk?"

"Sure," Jennifer said, walking to the chair next to her desk to sit down.

"Not here. Walk with me."

J.P. detected a note of fear in Mary's voice.

"Let's go out into the café and sit."

Mary looked left and right, as though she were being followed.

"It's no surprise to you that Jim and I are lovers, I'm sure."

J.P. nodded yes.

"I'm also a good friend of Lana. We play bridge together often. She's so sharp you'd think she was 30, not 90. I tell her things and she tells me things. Well, Lana asked me to stop seeing Jim."

J. P. was not surprised. Lana was not only an amateur sleuth, she also by nature someone who wanted to help protect her friends. Lana knew of Mary's heightened interest in sex. But Lana enjoyed her company and her wonderful stories of life and love. No one was more loyal than Mary to Lana. And she knew Mary also was loyal to Jim and would not tolerate words against him. So Lana didn't discourage her further.

But now Mary was revealing, her loyalty was being challenged.

"On many occasions Jim stays at my place. He says he loves how I've decorated it, first class all the way. He knows I used to decorate homes of many of my wealthy friends as well as my own. I love doing it. Now," she paused as though not sure she should confess this, "my very expensive engagement and wedding rings are missing from my safe place. I take them off at night, put them away. Jim has seen me do this many times. He's often kidded me about it saying if I ever went broke, selling those rings could bring in enough cash to guarantee my rent here for life."

"Do you feel disloyal to Jim telling me this now?"

"Yes, I do. I wouldn't except Lana told me to tell you and you'd know what to do. She told me to trust you. She does. You see Jim was with me the other night and as I prepared for bed I took my rings off and put them away in my safe place. He laughed and commented at my ritual that someday soon he'd have grander rings than mine. Now mine are gone."

J. P. sat, stunned. "Did you report this to police?"

"No, not yet. They are insured. I told Bob Redding and he asked me not to call the police just for a day or so. If they didn't turn up, as other missing things have, he'd help me file my report."

"Did you ask Jim about the rings?"

"I did. He was offended that I'd even ask him. I haven't been with him since. I decided never to have him in my place again."

"Mary, you must report this theft, and not to The Farm's security. Report it directly to the city police. Do not tell Bob or Jim what you have done."

Mary seemed to shrink into her chair. "I'm not sure I can. Bob thinks it will show up. Security is investigating he said."

"Do you trust them?"

"I must. They have been great so far."

"Then trust me. Lana does and now you must. Do not report this theft to Bob's men, only to the city police and do it now. Tell them the rings are gone and when you first noticed them missing, without actually accusing Jim. I think these recent thefts will be solved very soon."

Mary was uncomfortable, snitching on her lover. "I've have heard other women complain of missing expensive items of late, some who, shall we say, know Jim intimately? At a recent bridge game, a few said they found their missing jewelry and confessed and charged the missing jewelry to their occasional memory loss."

"That's good. But trust me on this. Your rings won't come back, of that I am sure."

The women got up, with Mary returning to the office, slumping at bit, J.P. thought, as she walked away. Mary genuinely liked Jim Ticknor. Now she doesn't trust him anymore. So she'd not only lost valuable rings but also someone she thought was a great lover and friend.

J.P. rushed back to the office to write some stories, but mentioned nothing in them about Mary's ring loss. She thought of Jim's last off hand remark to Mary that he was into something big and would soon move out of The Farm or perhaps out of the country.

He'd laughed, she said, reminding her he played the song "Don't Fence Me In" on air recently because, nibbling at her ear, "I never stay in any one place very long." Mary said "Funny guy." Now she told J.P. she no longer thinks he's funny.

The Farm was for her from the start a wonderful place to live, Mary told J.P., that's why she moved in. The Pleasant Hill Farm concept of an active lifestyle, whether in the fitness room or in bed, plus the mantra of live, love and laugh (Mary added lust after hooking up with Jim) kicked it up a notch when WOLD went on air.

The Farm was now America's prime address for affluent seniors. Redding and Ticknor proved to residents that life after 65 at The Farm could be active, rewarding, and fun. Aging was after all a normal life cycle, not a disease. Plus WOLD's often-zany volunteers were fast becoming legend.

Mary volunteered to be WOLD's receptionist even before she moved into one of the plush apartments on campus. She had married well two times, losing one husband to death and another to divorce. And Jim was right in his off hand comments about how Mary had acquired her wealth. Jewelry and stocks left her well off and easily able to afford retirement at The Farm.

Mary didn't grow up in a wealthy family. She did, however, have a remarkable pop music kind of singing voice since childhood. Her "stage mom" pushed her hard to start performing at an early age.

Mary loved performing songs from the Big Band era and sang professionally with local area bands. It was at one of those performances as a featured vocalist she met, dated, and then eventually married a prominent Cincinnati businessman who gave her the engagement and matching diamond rings she so cherished.

Actually even before Wayne Richardson's suspicious death and her missing ring incident, Mary had offered Jim a cash loan if he needed it.

They were in bed and he had told Mary he'd turned down the chance to go on a luxury cruise offered to all Farm residents. He confessed to Mary, "I just can't afford it."

Mary wanted him to go and would advance him the money. He refused, thanking her for her generosity and told her, "My low funds are only temporary. Soon that all will change."

Mary told J.P. she thought nothing of it then. Now, with her rings missing and Jim being suspected of taking it, she had to re-evaluate what their relationship was all about besides sex. Her conclusion was she had been used. That left her depressed, a state which only increased because now she also felt she'd thrown suspicion on a man she had worshipped for a short time.

Plus if J.P. suspicions proved fact and Wayne Richardson's death turned out to be murder, The Farm was about to hit the national news again, forever tainting the reputations of its two most prominent personalities.

CHAPTER 20 – Lana Knows

The study in Lana's penthouse held hundreds of photos of famous friends. None were of Wayne Richardson. In her early years of investing, she did meet him when she and Jim Ticknor joined Wayne in Bob's company that invested in many businesses. Bob even made money for her. But Wayne's dictatorial style turned Lana off, and she limited her socializing with Wayne to business and occasional cocktail parties. But lately Wayne called her more frequently to compare notes on what each knew that was damaging about their old partner Bob Redding. Lana clammed up. But she knew Wayne had a lot more on Bob than even she did and he wouldn't hesitate to use it to destroy him.

All media in the Greater Cincinnati area and TV news stations in Ohio went electric on news of the death of Wayne Richardson. He was a well-known political figure, womanizer and newsmaker. He also had more dirt on most politicians and would-be politicians than was ever disclosed, so no one dared to expose all his past affairs. Collectively, J.P. surmised, many politicos upon hearing of his death, finally exhaled.

He was rich, indulgent to those he liked and a tyrant and a feared enemy to those who crossed him. But he was dead, so his secrets died with him.

Honestly, J.P. thought, where does that leave her? She had no proof of anything illegal, only suspicions. Her Farm stories were just that, stories about people, her forte. Crime was not her beat.

Sylvia was beside herself hearing of Wayne's sudden death. Some on staff said he truly loved her. They had a long affair even though Wayne was Catholic and married. Staff gossip told Jennifer it was Wayne who convinced the Star-Times publisher Tyson Biggs, to elevate the hot reporter Sylvia to be the first editor of the new feature section, Leisure Plus. It wasn't long after that Sylvia broke it off with Wayne. Why? Rumor has it she preferred the company now of Star-Times publisher Tyson Biggs.

How to figure? J.P. personally thought her boss had a father-figure complex, picking men at least two decades older than she.

No one had really given J.P. the low down on why Wayne stayed at The Farm so often. What did he use his friend's apartment for besides big time poker games? Did he take women there?

Whatever he had on "the boys" had died with him. They'd had business dealings together in the past so if "the boys" were tainted, so was he.

No, J.P. reasoned, he had something new on them that he wanted to expose, for what -- revenge? And due to lack of evidence, had her hot story flat-lined for lack of proof of any of her suspicions?

What does Lana really know? She's a dear friend already and remains a gold mine for new stories mostly about her past and whom she knows. She knew just about every one in the entertainment business for decades. But how well did she know Wayne Richardson, J.P. asked herself. He was big in Cincinnati, and Lana's just... big everywhere.

J.P. decided to play out the cards before the deck went cold. She called Lana for her reaction to Wayne's "natural" death.

"He was a dirt bag, honey," Lana told me. "Sure, he had more money than most. Almost more than me, but that didn't make him a gentleman. He was a user. Play his game and you got crowned. Deny or cross him, and it's check-mate."

"Where were you on his hit list?"

"Well, honey, you can guess I'm not one to be used. If there is any of that using to be done, I'm doing it. Call us equals. He knew it and so did I. I give as much as I get. But I also care about people. Wayne didn't. Oh, the stories I could tell you about him would make even an experienced reporter like you gasp."

Now that's the best teaser J.P. had heard all day. It's time to mine story gold through Lana, she thought.

J.P. said: "When may I come see you again? Our police reporters are mopping up the Wayne story so I'm on my own. I have something to tell you, too, about Wayne, that you might not know."

"Honey, there is nothing about Wayne I don't know. I pay good money to know."

"Maybe. Maybe not. When?"

"We've done so many lunches I've gained 10 pounds. How about a hot toddy for the body instead say around 4 today?"

Rats, she thought. What about Paul and her date for tonight? Maybe she should flip a coin, heads Lana and tails Paul? Heads Lana. Tails, Paul?

Lana won. J.P.'s educated gut prevailed over her heart. Only Lana could solve her mystery now.

"Lana, sometime after four I'll be there." It has to be Lana, Jennifer thought, because she's J.P.'s job security. She added, "And if you have any clippings or background on the boys I'd sure like to see them now."

Paul, dear Paul, Jennifer thought, we seem to be star crossed. This story is going down a whole new path and...and let's face, J.P thought, she is a pathfinder.

Que Sera, Sera, Paul.

* * *

It is hard to explain to a woman like Lana that you don't drink. For her drinking was a way of life, and to some extent, still is. But my refusing her "hot toddy for the body" again and again was not a way into her good graces. But J.P. finally convinced her because of her severe allergy to alcohol drinks were deadly. Finally, that subject was dropped forever.

"Well, honey, I suspect you can't do anything about that allergy so I forgive you. I'll have my gal Friday whip up tea and snacks instead now. How's that?"

"Tea is fine. I love it. And as promised here's my info on Wayne. Just after being hired at the Star-Times I had several mysterious phone calls at work and home from a man I called the whisperer. They were anonymous from this man who claimed to have the goods on Jim Ticknor and Bob Redding, new information that would be more than be just embarrassing, perhaps criminal."

She watched Lana. A student of body language, J.P. knew it reveals far more at times than words. Lana didn't flinch. It seemed as though she inwardly sighed though, as if saying to herself, Wayne was out to hurt people again and whoever it was, they got to him first.

Lana put down her elegant teacup enhanced with spirits and said, "So?"

J.P tried to shock Lana into revelations. "Well, as it turns out my mystery caller, was Wayne Richardson. I had an appointment to get information he said was urgent. I went to the apartment where he said to meet him. I rang. He didn't answer the door at 707 because unknown to me then, he was already dead. They didn't discover the body right away because the resident was out of the country and someone hung a door sign at 707 saying "Do Not Disturb.""

"So?"

God, does nothing surprise her, J.P. thought.

"Lana, is there anything criminal in businesses that involved Jim and Bob that you know about?"

There. It was out.

"No," she said, but cautiously. This time there was a slight hesitation in her voice. That was an opening.

"I thought you knew everything about everybody here. Are you saying they are clean in their entire joint enterprises?"

"What I am saying, dear J.P., is I did have them investigated before I invested with them. I kept those reports which had some puzzling information in them. The boys and I were silent partners way back in that California talent agency. Yes, I threw some money at that enterprise, but I didn't get hurt when it failed.

"Later the boys were frequently my guests at my old Cincinnati supper clubs. That led to closer business ties later on. And while we were financially active, they were clean. I had put money into that talent agency fiasco as a friend, and then got out before it went belly up. But the boys didn't get hurt either."

"Lana, remember when Paul and I visited you?"

"Who could forget that beautiful man? Why haven't you landed him? Were I 60 years younger, you wouldn't have a chance."

J.P. laughed. Lana was such a treat.

"Paul and I are old friends."

"Honey, if there is one thing I've learned in my ninety years on earth and after all those marriages and many encounters of an intimate kind is that men and women are never just friends. Either they're on you or they are off, if you know what I mean."

"Lana, you make me blush."

"Honey, I doubt I could. You've been reporting far too long."

"Why did Jim Ticknor really come to The Farm, Lana? I know you agreed to live here to help Bob establish The Farm among the affluent as the place to go in retirement. I know he hoped to bring in the richest clientele possible from all over the country, many of who were show business retirees and your friends. And initially his mission was so good because he truly did believe older people should be recognized as active, involved people just as they were when young."

J.P. paused to allow her words to sink in. This was no time for an ambush. She was not questioning Lana's motives to move to The Farm.

"Why did he bring Jim aboard now? This retired lifestyle isn't Jim's thing. He's more for those big lights of Broadway, casinos, yachts, women."

Lana reluctantly put down her enhanced tea.

"Honey, if it's one thing I've learned living this good long life is that no matter how wonderful life is, it changes with age. Every part in our bodies eventually changes and, hell, often collapses. Even Jim knew that. That's why he got out of New York. He was 66 and fading fast on TV. Besides, these days, no one wants to hire a senior news anchor or commercial broadcaster who will soon push 70, even one with a full head of hair and a wallet that never closes."

Reporter J.P. responded: "So Jim decided on retirement and a volunteer job at a little FM radio station with nothing in it for him but hard work and perhaps a little more notoriety? That's kind of hard to believe."

"Well, remember a big fish in a small pond is better than no pond at all, honey. Besides, there are lots of wealthy females here. And again he is a celebrity at WOLD. Women still flock to him. Many with diamonds on both hands. And a little of that kindness and dedication that exudes from those everyday WOLD volunteers perhaps have rubbed off on him. It sure has on me. Those volunteers have such amazing stories. They are better on air than all that on those phony soap operas on TV. WOLD volunteers are dedicated. The station in return gives them a reason to get up in the morning."

Lana gave a deep sigh.

"Mary comes up here and keeps me up to date on all the news, good, bad, even evil. I tell her insights, she gives me gossip. Then I let my money do my talking for me, always behind the scenes. I confess I am a big contributor to WOLD."

No surprise there, J.P. thought.

"So you think volunteerism really has worked for Jim? That he didn't come here with another direct purpose in mind?"

Lana hesitated. Then, "Knowing him, he probably did, yes, but he perhaps to his own surprise he found some goodness here and is trying to absorb it in his own way."

Change of subject.

"Lana, is The Farm a cover for any illegal enterprises for Jim or Bob or both, do you think?"

Lana reached for the brandy sitting on the antique marble table to enliven her tea. The diamond ring she wore on her little finger glistened. There was an awkward silence.

"What I am about to tell you, J.P is off the record, for now. Can you honor that?"

"That's my stock in trade. I can, and will. Point me in the right direction is all I ask."

"You know we've had some supposedly minor, random robberies lately, largely unreported to police? They are far more serious than you or anyone knows. There are many residents here who have had expensive items taken from their cottages and apartments, including mine. Items that are worth a lot. Bob knows this but never acted on it, always asking for a little more time.

"Most items are highly insured. So Bob is trying to keep those residents from reporting the losses publicly for now. Surprisingly some later were found even though their owners swear they were gone from their apartments. It was as if some items were taken, appraised, and some returned. Bob says he's on it. But my own detectives told me more details. Don't ask how they know. That's what I pay them big bucks to find out.

"There was one famous painting now missing but was not reported. It happens to be mine, a Picasso, my favorite. Taken from my apartment on the day we had a fire here. And only Bob and I know it is real, not a reproduction."

"Oh my God, Lana, you've been robbed?"

"Quiet. Friday is in the kitchen. She's scared of everything."

"Maybe she's in on it?"

"Friday? Never. She's been with me thirty years."

"Whom do you suspect?"

"Someone in Farm security working with Bob's knowledge. A master key is located in security, but locked up and given out only with Bob's permission. This young new security guy my detectives think is part of a gang or some group Bob knows about or maybe even directs. The items already missing were worth a lot of money. The ones returned were put back, my guys think, to throw residents off track, doubt their own memories and buy the thieves time. A set up. But things taken, and kept, were selective pieces. The thief or thieves knew what to take, what to leave behind or return. But only Bob knew my painting was not a reproduction."

J.P. gasped.

"My detectives think that new young security guard was in on that first haul, with help and direction of Bob. The guard wouldn't know a Picasso from a Petty girl drawing, in my opinion.

"So my guys say he was coached as to what to take. Then apparently he has passed along the most valuable things to the gang's mastermind. Strangely, though, nothing stolen so far has shown up in pawnshops, as far as my guys know. Of course Bob asked residents not to make police reports just yet, apparently to buy time for what, I don't know. One thing for sure, my Picasso has not surfaced."

She paused, sipping again her laced tea, observing Jennifer as much as Jennifer was observing her, who now felt Lana knew a lot more about the robberies than she was revealing. Lana suspicions about Bob deeply troubled her, J.P. observed, because as she had considered him her friend for such a long time.

"Bob told me to give him a few days before calling in the police and alerting the insurance companies. He told me he knew or had suspicions about the thefts, and he and his security team would mop it up. But the problem is Bob and some of his security men I think are involved, my guys believe, and they are ready to strike again soon, and then disappear. They know for a fact Bob renewed his passport."

Jennifer stopped writing. Lana knew who was committing the thefts. But did she also suspect they killed Wayne, too? And why?

Lana went on: "My men think Jim also is involved. He's short on cash and in the past went on board with Bob whenever there was a chance for a killing. After all the master key to all homes and apartments rests with Bob, and unless someone in security stole it or duplicated it, Bob orchestrated how and when to get into targeted cottages and apartments. Bob knows the Farm is a miniature Fort Knox.

"My guys think the real target is me. Why me? I hate to tell you how much I keep here in cash in my wall safe, besides all my jewelry. Whoever took my Picasso knows my apartment and is hungry for the bigger prize. And how did that thief who took my painting know it was real? Only Bob knew unless he passed that information out to others accidentally or on purpose. My agency thinks the big one is soon."

"Who are your detectives?"

"If I tell you, their cover is blown and they'd have to kill you."

She laughed aggravating that throaty cough. She waved J.P. off, indicating not to worry. "Honey, the doctor who told me this cough will kill me is long gone himself. He treated old age as a disease, instead of honoring it as life's final cycle. I fired him. Now he's dead and I'm still alive and kicking."

She sipped her 90 proof tea. "No, my boys are trustworthy and well paid. We've set a trap. We'll catch them soon. We know they plan to rob me then pull out. If our plan works you'll be the first to know. And with Wayne's death bringing such notoriety here, whoever is planning the big one knows he or they must strike quickly now."

J.P. anxiety heightened. Her gut, always reliable, said, this is it. She had to ask, "When will I know your plan?" she asked.

"Soon, honey, very, very soon. Now drink your tea. I have to pee."

She got up and rushed out of the room. J.P. was flushed, and speechless.

So Lana was very much involved, J. P. said to herself. She believes she's the final target. How she knew she did not share with J.P. other than she relies on her private detectives.

She had said she suspected the new security guy was involved in the Picasso theft because he had been coming up too often to do security checks in her apartment. She called Bob once and he assured her it had to be done in every apartment, not just hers.

Lana came back into the room with her hand extended. That meant an automatic goodbye.

But J.P. had to ask again: "When is your plan coming down? What will you do?"

Lana nodded her head no, repeating. "Just soon, honey. Soon. Goodbye, for now."

J.P. tried to stall, to say anything to stay a bit longer, but Lana would have none of it. When Lana is finished talking, J.P. told herself, zip it up. Leave. So she did.

But what she felt in her always reliable gut was she should stay with her dear friend Lana a while longer, especially this particular night.

CHAPTER 21 – Heroes

Jennifer's adrenalin rush depleted as she opened her front door. All day she'd feel exhilaration and fear, pumping her up. The biggest fear now was for her new friend whom she now loved, Lana Koppler. Generous beyond belief, but tough as nails when necessary, the philanthropist to Jennifer was a hero to rich and poor and all those in between. Lana's need to always be on top of everything worried J.P. Perhaps Lana placed too much trust in her detective agency. Did her long successes in dealing with major and minor problems blindside her to the real dangers from her former friends?

When she put the key in the lock of her condo, Jennifer was tired, ready for bed. The day had been wild, but to a reporter like herself, fascinating as well. She didn't want it to end, but now admitted to herself that her middle-aged body cried out to knock it off and get some sleep.

But who stood inside before her but Paul, beautiful Paul. Only now there was a worried look on his handsome face.

Why is Paul in my living room, she thought? Where is her Trish? What the hell is going on here? All these questions bombarded the tired reporter.

When Paul wrapped his arms around her she stopped questioning and just absorbed the moment, decades in coming.

"Here, sit down," he said bringing her to the couch beside him. Then, somewhat like a puzzled benevolent parent, he asked, "What is going on over there at The Farm?"

"You heard it on the news?"

"Of course. I wrapped up my business in Columbus, and I came down to talk to you. Are you into something over your head? I have that gut feeling you needed me. That's why I'm here."

J.P. laughed. Her gladiator. It is a couple of decades, late, my dear friend, she thought. Still --welcome.

Instead she answered, "Paul, I am not sure but there is a bigger story at The Farm other than the Richardson death, which apparently was recorded as natural, even though I am not so sure of that. I think he had the goods on someone, he and his intruder scuffled in a plan, and Wayne's heart gave out. Anyway, it's not a murder on the books. And yes, he was my whisperer, the contact man who I was supposed to get information from, but didn't. His death left that story hanging."

He put his arm around J.P. She went on, more to sort her own now scattered thoughts than to explain them.

"But there is a new development with Lana I am pursuing, which kind of frightens me tonight."

"Lana? How does she fit into the picture?"

"More than anyone knows. But she's cagey. And with her money, she reveals only what she wants to reveal. Beyond that I can't say. It is off the record. I promised."

That Paul understood. He was always one of the ethical reporters, who, when someone trusted him with a secret, it stayed that way. They had that in common.

"You look bushed."

Great, Jennifer thought. That's what a woman loves to hear when standing before her is her dream man.

"I am. And ready to call it day. I'm sorry I had to cancel our date."

"I know you. If there is a story, that gets the number one priority. I get it. I just wish we had more time. You and I are the only people I know who can communicate exactly where we left off 20 years ago. I don't want to lose that, ever again."

Jennifer thought, boy, me either. It sent a jolt through her of renewal like nothing else could.

"Tell you what. I'll leave you for now. I'm just going to stick around town for a couple of days more, out of your way. Maybe I can help you with this new breaking story. I'll leave with you and Trish where I'll be staying at the house of a friend here. Here's the telephone numbers where you can reach me, anytime. It's your call."

Jennifer thought she could have squeezed him to death at that moment. But damn it, she thought, middle-aged tiredness again intervened. Instead she accepted reality, waved him goodbye and he left.

She went to bed alone. Barely audible she said to herself, "Damn it!"

* * *

Jennifer's phone awakened her at 4 a.m. It was Lana's Friday, and she was crying.

"J.P., You gotta come over here. Miss Lana needs you. I can't tell you nothin' more. Just come, alone. No cops, Miss Lana says."

She hung up.

At first J.P thought she needed to awaken Trish. Instead she opted to leave her a note, telling her exactly where she was going and giving her Lana's telephone number. But remembering Friday's warning issued from Lana not to tell anyone where she was going, she told Trish only to call at Lana's in case of a real emergency.

Then she raced out of her condo. No one, friend of foe, calls anyone else at 4 a.m. unless it is a serious emergency. She could hardly breathe.

J.P. couldn't get to Lana's apartment fast enough. It wasn't far but it seemed like hours to her before she arrived at her door, tapped on it quietly and Friday opened it, expecting her. She had on a long nightgown. Her eyes were stuck on wide-open. Her look was that of pure fear.

"Miss Lana is in her bedroom. Please to follow."

All of Lana's lights in her huge sitting room-bedroom were on. Lana was in her king-sized bed that was adorned by satin sheets. Her usually highly coffered hair was a mess. But that isn't what frightened J.P. Lana's right eye was badly bruised, as was her face.

"Lana... what the?

"Come closer J.P. and sit here on my bed. I've had Friday help me back to bed, after she cleaned things up. I need to be alone with you." A deep breath followed, then exhaling all air from her lungs. She was fighting for calm.

She shuddered. Then she let it out: "I've been raped, brutalized ... and robbed."

J.P. couldn't utter a sound. It was too unbelievable. She thought, I'm talking to a ninety-year-old woman who was raped?

"The man was partially hooded and masked, but he knew me, my apartment, and where everything was. He was after the special contents of my secret wall safe. See there, where that picture is ajar?"

She pointed to the wall.

"That safe is empty. The rapist told me to stay quiet. I had gone to bed early, took a sleeping pill as I do sometimes, so I was out of it. But for some reason I awakened mid-morning, probably to pee, or because I heard something. Apparently what awakened me was the clang of my metal cash box dropping down outside of my safe. The robber first emptied the contents and dropped it. I had perhaps a million in cash, gold and jewelry."

She gulped in more air to try to expand her lungs. J.P. just stared at her, but still could not utter a sound.

Lana continued, "I guess I gasped out loud, realizing what was happening. The robber rushed over to me, put his hand over my mouth and said, 'Shut up. Don't move. I'm out of here and you are to stay put and silent until I do. Or you die. Get it?'

"I was too frightened to speak so I nodded yes.

"He went back to the wall safe, put the box and other items into his large cloth bag. I then instinctively and foolishly tried to reach for my phone. Apparently he saw me. Damn that night-light I've always insisted stay on. He rushed over to me, knocked down the phone, and dragged me partially out of my bed, striking me in face. I screamed. That's when he raped me."

She inhaled, slowly, deeply. She was less frightened than outraged. How could someone do that to a ninety-year-old woman? Why? Why?

"J.P., this guy didn't expect me to wake up. He apparently knew where my hidden safe was and thought he'd be in and out before I woke up. He had to be a professional safe cracker to break that lock's code. He apparently was hired just for this job. Only a real pro worked that fast. Only Bob Redding knows I even have this wall safe. And I am the only one who knows how to open it. But that masked guy wasn't Bob. That I know. Yet he knew exactly where to go and how to open my safe and did it all silently. He was an expert."

She spoke so rapidly now J.P. feared she'd expire.

"I don't know why he attacked me but I guess maybe because I screamed. Or maybe revenge on the rich? Who knows? Maybe it was his way to put me down?"

She rattled on after taking another rapid deep breath and being now somewhat incoherent. But Jennifer didn't dare interfere.

"Look at me, a shriveled up old skeleton. There's nothing sexy about me. But rape is never about sex. It is about dominance. It was to show his power over me. He was no killer or I wouldn't be here now talking to you. I think he knew all about me, hated and resented me."

She couldn't stop talking. That was OK since J.P. couldn't speak anyway. In her mind was that searing question: who would ever attack a ninety-year-old woman? What accumulation of hate was there in another human being to do that kind of criminal act? Did he intend to rape? Or was he really there to kill thus silence her?

J.P. mentally tried to put the puzzle together without words. She remembered her personal unproved theory that Wayne Richardson's heart gave out on him only after a confrontation with someone who knew he had a weak heart. It had to be someone in Security because Jennifer told security the day Wayne died she would later visit that cottage at 707. So Security knew the day, date and time of that interview with Wayne. Who in Security was it she'd talked to that day? Oh, yes, oh, God, that tall, young security guard. So did she actually tip him off and allow him time to go to Wayne and silence him?

J.P. could not ask Lana anything. So Lana rambled on. In her mind Jennifer wondered if this robber-rapist also was Wayne's assassin and who, after Lana woke up and surprised him, decided to silence Lana as well? The fact he knew where Lana's safe was and what to take was terrifying.

Lana's words from moments ago rang out again loud and clear in Jennifer's brain. "Rape is not about sex, it's about the power of one person over another."

To anyone else who was Lana's age such an attack probably would have killed her instantly. Maybe he intended to do just that. But was it on someone's orders?

Lana spoke as though she'd just read J.P. questioning mind.

"J.P., I knew this guy even though he was masked. I'm sure it was that young security guard and apparently he's no killer. But he had a knife, and threatened to use it. In my younger years I could have kicked him into soprano-hood. But all I could do was silently cry during the attack."

She heaved a new sob out loud.

J.P. joined her.

"Stop, J.P. I think of you as a dear friend and because I won't report this rape, you have to help me catch this guy, and his vicious gang, if there is one. My team was so close to solving this case without violence. I had jewelry and cash in that safe. He knew exactly where to go and showed himself an expert in how to get into my apartment and into my safe and get it open -- fast. Had I not cooperated, I wouldn't be alive now to tell you about it. I am surprised he let me live. But I'm also sure smart isn't in his tool bag."

"Lana," J.P. said, finally gathering her voice, "What am I to do? This rape must be reported. And you need a doctor."

"Honey, a doctor I'll get. Mine. But report the rape? Never. The robbery? You bet. My detectives will get to the bottom of it today with police. They already are on it. I called them. But I want you to know the whole story just in case I expire so you can be there when they catch all of his gang, which now I am sure there is."

"Whom do you suspect?"

"You know, Bob. We learned Bob hired that new security guard probably for his skill to be able to quickly break into my safe. Bob knows all about my safe's location. No one else does. And that same guard was my rapist, I'm sure. Same size, same blond hair, even though he was partially hooded and masked. But he is not the brain of this robbery. He has limited amounts of those or he'd never have let me live.

"Not even my Friday knows about my safe's location or its contents. A stranger to this apartment could never find my safe that quickly. He knew the location right off and was able to get into it quickly. That means he also had a key to get in and knew to turn off my alarm system. Bob hires or signs off on all security staff, hand picks them. My men believe I was always their main target all along. But the rape was not planned."

She couldn't stop talking. Jennifer couldn't stop listening. She remained silent.

"I had to tell Bob when I wanted to install that wall safe, to get permission to tear up that wall. And lately this security guy kept coming up here to my apartment on several pretenses.

"My wealth is known. That isn't news. But the location of my safe is privileged information. My team already is on it this moment. No one else knows yet, except you and Friday. And she's pissing scared, poor thing. I've faced death more times than she's ever recovered from frights."

Her calmness and deliberate actions amazed me. She was even now deliberate in her plan to capture the thief, thieves or gang.

Her face was a mess, swelling now. Her eye was black.

"What actually happened before tonight that you told your detectives but didn't tell me? Something was in the wind, wasn't it? It was part of Wayne's urgent message he wanted to get to me, wasn't it? He knew they were out to get you? He had information?"

She took a deep breath.

"I had a call from a well known New York art and fine jewelry dealer. Wayne knew this, too, but how, I don't know. Someone, the dealer said, in Cincinnati called him long distance to inquire about selling a painting, my missing Picasso. That dealer knew that painting was legally mine. He said he keeps track of owners of fine art. So, since it wasn't me or someone saying they represented me, he became suspicious. So he called me. He said a man named Roland Tresh had made the call to him saying he wanted to help settle a friend's estate. The friend owned a Picasso that he wanted to sell."

"Oh, Lana, no, was it Ticknor?" I gasped.

She nodded her head yes, then quickly added, "My agency ran a check on that call and yes, and it was Jim trying to fence my painting. I guess that was his job as part of Bob's plan."

She also said her "guys" were ready to close in today. They did not think Bob would be so brazen as to rob her in the middle of the night. They'd no doubt wait until she went to a specific event or program such as today's scheduled appointment at the campus beauty salon and spa, part of her regular routine.

To herself J.P. asked, did Lana's detectives know who had done those other robberies? And if Jim and Bob are in on this whole plan, did they also order Lana's rape, thinking she'd not survive such an attack? Or was the safe cracker just so enraged by this old woman's wealth he wanted to decimate her any way he could? Did he hate the rich that much?

Lana, amazingly composed now, said she didn't think the rape was planned or that initially the robber intended to harm her. He was so sure of himself because he had prior knowledge of things that he thought he could get in and out before she awoke. He didn't count on her waking up. They could make a clean get away before anyone was awake. Then Bob, his entourage, and maybe even Jim, would be long gone.

Lana said only Bob knew Lana took sleeping pills, even to picking them up for her once. Besides, she added, her attacker was young and impulsive. She had awakened while he was in the process of emptying the safe, and she surprised him, so he ad-libbed his crime from there.

"Yes, I admit to you that for some time my detectives, and Wayne, knew Bob and Jim, were part of an international theft ring, and have been, for some time. Both Bob and Jim for years have been invited into the homes of the rich and famous so they can get information that his international gang could use. They were the inside guys, we think. This young security guy was the last one hired by Bob to be his inside guy for this robbery. His credentials must have included expert safe cracking. My agency guys think he gave his loot to Bob to allow it to cool off.

"The boys have been partners and suspected in other white-collar crimes for years, but never caught, so I'm not surprised at this. I didn't tell you that I, along with the late Wayne Richardson, had proof of some of Jim and Bob's past activities.

"For example, Bob keeps two sets of WOLD books here at The Farm. One is for the IRS and trustees, another set for himself. He has sole control of WOLD's finances. In a fit of anger recently in talking to Bob I mentioned my and Wayne's evidence on them, suggesting whatever he was up to at The Farm must cease and that he should resign but before he did, return my painting. I didn't report it because I knew who had it. For many years I never thought anyone could corrupt Bob. He's a genius. Apparently an evil one.

"I know it is hard to believe, J.P., but there it is. Those reports on my boys were in that safe, too. They are gone along with my cash and jewels."

She sighed again, even deeper this time. Then the cough erupted. J.P. was alarmed. Lana couldn't stop talking.

"I'm frightened, now. I never thought I'd be hurt. My detectives were so close. But I don't think that attack on me was ordered by anyone. It just happened out of rage, stupidity and pure hatred. Maybe it also was to prove he was in charge."

She began shaking now. But talking seemed to help so J.P. remained silent.

Jennifer eased off the bed and sank into a plush beige velvet chair at Lana's bedside. She still couldn't speak.

"J.P., don't report any of this, not yet. Let the FBI and my detectives wait out for that painting sale to be negotiated today, along with anything else they try to sell or promise to sell, such as my jewelry. Then the FBI will pounce, aided by my detective agency, rounding up all the parties with concrete proof.

"But hear me on this. Not a word about the rape to anyone. Ever. Your word? My detectives are all former cops and I'm not sure what they'd do if they knew. They knew I was roughed up, but not raped. No one but you, and me, know what really happened here tonight. They think it was robbery and I got roughed up because I woke up during it."

Finally J.P. found her voice. "Lana, my God, you are 90 years old. You need medical attention. And I promised myself long ago always report a rape. It's a crime."

"How do you think I got to be 90? I'm still tough as nails. I might die today, but not from that rape. Honey, I've had far worse happen to me. It's just that now, in the December of my life, this is perhaps is the most humiliating thing ever. It is almost too much for these old bones."

"What do you want me to do? Please tell me."

"Call your friend Paul. He's a straight shooter; I've had him checked out, too. *(My God, she checks out everybody, Jennifer thought.)* He could help us because my team thinks Bob and Jim have been hooked up with this international gang for some time. We know Jim needs money. He always does. As for Bob, he's greedy. Perhaps Paul has heard of their international jewelry gang?"

She rambled on. J.P. wasn't talking, still breathless.

"It's big. Too big for me. Besides, we need a witness to everything from here on in, to get it all down and confirm it all. And it might even be dangerous to you now that you know these are no local thieves, J.P. They are big with no scruples. That dealer who called me was from New York. He won't touch anything that's hot. He reported Jim's call because Jim on the phone sounded phony and identified himself as a former New Yorker who knew about this dealer's reputation to buy expensive things. After the dealer hung up he contacted the police."

Finally Jennifer's head began to work. Yes, she thought, this could be very dangerous. If Jim and Bob had hooked up with international thieves, they'd stop at nothing to succeed, or to cover their tracks.

Lana was alive because it was still dark and she didn't resist the robber-rapist. What if he came back to finish her off—on orders because she saw him? And if he didn't talk, no one in his gang would know about the rape, including Bob. But unless there was quick action to apprehend them, they all will soon be gone.

Suddenly J.P. feared for her daughter, Trish, and, yes, herself. And now, if she allowed him to participate, Paul.

"Lana, I love you. But I can't put Paul in harm's way, too. Yes, he does have a lot of connections internationally as he's a crack newsman, and he's a good man. But I can't jeopardize his life with this. Let's keep it between you and me, the FBI and your detectives."

Lana sat straight up. "No, we need your Paul. (Jennifer thought: my Paul?) They do. And we have to let someone else know what is going on. They won't suspect Paul's inquiries. He has sources and can check this gang out quickly and quietly with them."

Jennifer couldn't argue with the logic but for the first time in her career, she felt afraid.

"Lana, what can I do to help you, right now, this minute?"

"Friday takes care of me, even though right now she's so frightened she can't stop shaking. She did not hear my scream sleeping in her quarters on the other side of my apartment. And she does not realize I was raped. She saw I had been roughed up and I told her I fell out of bed. Now I hurt, and my face is a mess, I'm sure. But makeup will cover most of that. We do need to act quickly though. Can you stay with me?"

Jennifer said she'd call her daughter to tell her that Lana was ill and she needed her to stay for rest of the night and day. Then she'd call Paul, and pray he'd understand.

He not only did, but also said he would cooperate and yes, immediately said he would disavow any ownership of this big story that was unraveling, other than helping J.P. as deep background. She explained Lana's fears and her strong suspicions about who was behind it all. He said all the more reason he wanted in on the arrest. He liked Lana.

It all came to a head sooner than any expected.

CHAPTER 22 – To Catch A Thief

Over a long newspaper and writing career, Jennifer met all sorts of people. Some were heroic, some were average, a few criminal and despicable.

Once an old college friend of Jennifer's called her to ask for help. The woman admitted she was in a deep depression. Her mother had been raped and police had not found the rapist. Her mother lived in a swank apartment building during a particularly hot Cincinnati summer. When her air conditioning failed, the mother opened her bedroom window before retiring. The rapist entered, raped, robbed and killed her. The friend said so far he' d not been caught.

Jennifer called in a lot of favors and police reopened the cold case. That led to the arrest of the rapist-killer and a life in prison.

Too late.

Jennifer's college friend committed suicide, a second one to further scar her soul.

Early morning Lana receive another call from the New York art dealer.

He'd reported to police and then the FBI the recent inquiry about a Picasso with a promise of expensive jewelry to come. Since he knew

the art was not a legal sale, and there was an offer of jewelry as well, he quickly alerted the authorities. The police and the FBI were involved and a team was flying in to Cincinnati immediately to close in today.

Then Lana, exhausted, fell asleep in her bed. Jennifer did likewise in her chair.

Later on Lana offered J.P. the use of her apartment to become more presentable. Her guest bathroom was amazing and she enjoyed the luxury of it all, trying to make her mind go blank for a while as she showered. Then she dressed quickly.

Lana took a long time before she came out of her master bath, looking almost normal. She was a beauty, more inside than out these days, to be sure, but a beauty nonetheless.

J.P. decided at that moment she loved that old lady. Lana helped so many people anonymously. Not many knew about her vast good works, except for her accountants. She was a true role model.

When the FBI finished their interviews with Lana she had Friday order in food in for all. No one was hungry. But all consumed great quantities of coffee.

Lana told no one about the rape. It was her secret, and Jennifer's--forever. Not even Paul knew. Jennifer vowed she'd kept her word although it went against her grain. Rape s a major crime and must be reported. Always. No exceptions. That was her promise to herself as a reporter and a female human being. But now, again, someone she cared about refused to do so. Carolyn did in her past, too. Now

Lana. How Lana has survived this brutal and horrific act at her age J.P. did not know, but she has so far.

Lana said she would die with that secret of being a rape victim. How could J.P. refuse her? If she reported it, Lana would just deny it happened, of that J.P. was sure. So with great sorrow and deeply felt emotion, J.P. forced herself to remain silent even though doing so wrenched her gut.

Now Lana wanted, actually felt, she must, tell her friend Jennifer the details of her assault, details that would be buried when she was.

Lana agonized over the fact that she wasn't able to reach her apartment's emergency cord and silently call for help. Her audible gasp at seeing the robber at her safe is what gave her away to the thief. He knew also she now was a witness.

"Bob not only knew where my safe was, he was aware I took sleep medication. So he must have told the intruder that he could crack the safe, empty its contents and get out easily, all while I slept. He'd be gone before I woke up. My pill's failure to completely knock me out proved him wrong."

Jennifer felt uncomfortable listening to Lana's account of the rape, but she knew Lana needed to tell it just once out loud to someone. She wanted it heard, and then forgotten.

"The rapist ran to my bed, dragged me off by the hair. He smacked me, hard, saying 'Rich bitches like you don't deserve any mercy.' There was pure hate in his voice. He wanted to humiliate me. On the floor he kneeled over me, pulled up my gown. I thought his thrust would kill me. But I remained motionless and silent. He left quickly after that. I must have blacked out for a few moments, then I half-pulled myself up and yelled long and hard this time for Friday. She helped me back into my bed, thinking I'd fallen out, but so shaken I thought she'd faint right there."

She coughed, a hard heave followed. J.P. silently prayed this would not be the time she was to die.

Then clearing her throat, she spoke again, "In a way I rescued Friday from a brutal household when she was a teen. She knows abuse first hand. I gave her a job as housekeeper and she grew into being my favorite person and companion. There is nothing she wouldn't do for me, and I feel the same way about her. Because she came from a family where there was major violence, I don't want her ever to know her benefactor was also sexually assaulted. Do you hear me, J.P.?"

Lana later did get medical attention for her black eye and bruises from her private physician, who was always on call when needed. J.P. was sure he was on a hefty retainer to be available at a moment's notice.

What did Lana tell him to explain what happened to her Jennifer could only speculate. But the doctor didn't report the rape because Lana didn't tell him it happened. Nor did J.P. report it, even though every fiber of her being cried out for it to be known and the rapist caught and punished.

Over the years Jennifer had covered many stories before involving rape, but never was there reported one on a woman Lana's age. It was unbelievable.

But it was her story to verify. And she was not talking.

CHAPTER 23 – Retribution

Never had Jennifer thought after her divorce and moving her and Trish to Cincinnati she would be find a new life. She'd settle for shaking off the old one. She wasn't sure she could trust another man ever again. It didn't matter, she told herself, as there is no happy ever after. So she concentrated on launching Trish into adulthood and regaining her confidence as a top reporter on a metropolitan newspaper. She found new friends, old and young. She grew as a person, realizing how valuable elders were in her life. Then the unexpected happened. Her soul mate showed up after a twenty plus year hiatus. It was too late. Or was it?

Once Lana's detective agency men were on the scene with the FBI and Paul, things moved rapidly.

They wanted the leader, first. So they rushed to Bob Redding's apartment, knowing he might flee out of the country with his loot if they didn't.

Bob's door was locked. Police and FBI pounded on it, demanding Bob open up. When he didn't they kicked it open.

Guns drawn, they advanced into his large apartment, but he wasn't there. They rushed to his bedroom, no Bob. Then they approached a locked door, apparently Bob's home office. Locked. One officer kicked it open, stepped back. There were gasps.

Bob was limp, hanging there, twisting from a rope. His high ceiling allowed him to throw a rope over a beam to hang himself.

No one said a word. Then someone commanded, "Cut him down."

Paul and detectives walked over to a large desk. On top were several bags full of money, jewels, gold coins and next to the desk below, a packed suitcase.

Bob's wall safe was open. Police pulled back the wrapping from a small painting on the desk to reveal Lana's Picasso. Bob's flight tickets were on the desk.

Apparently Bob had planned to flee that morning right after Lana's robbery, but when his safe cracker delivered the final loot to him and told him Lana had awakened before he could get out, he'd left a witness.

Bob apparently realized his time had run out. Rather than face arrest, his Plan B was to end his own life.

Lana's team, Paul, police and the FBI virtually ran next to Jim's nearby apartment, leaving others to attend to the suicide and cleanup. Jim was still in bed. Apparently he didn't plan to leave with Bob but would join him later to avoid suspicion.

Jim was true to form. A late sleeper, the police forcibly entered his apartment, found him still in bed, surprisingly alone.

"What the hell..." Paul recounted to J.P. later. Jim loudly protested the forced entry.

"Get up, Mr. Ticknor, you are under arrest for grand theft," Paul told him.

Paul reported that Jim ran his hand through his ample hair, trying to straighten up. Even in crisis, Jim needed to look good.

"Gentleman, you are mistaken. Do you know who I am?"

Paul couldn't resist. "I do. You and your friend Bob are criminals of long standing and were bleeding The Farm to death. Add to that the criminal assault on your friend Lana."

"What? I know nothing of any assault on Lana." Paul said that seemed genuine. Jim was in on the robberies but apparently didn't sign on to hurting Lana. That was the thief's on-the-spot decision, first roughing her up and then (unreported) the rape, which no one knew about, done out of his own hatred of the rich.

Appearance being the only rule Jim felt important to him at that moment, the police allowed him quickly to dress. Paul noted Jim groomed and checked himself out in his mirror. Never know where there will be a photographer, was Jim's mantra.

He was marched out from The Farm handcuffed, accompanied by camera flashings and an army of media demanding some responses. They got none. Jim smiled for the cameras. No one at that moment told him Bob committed suicide.

* * *

Within days of the attack, the security officer-robber-rapist and a few dirty security guards also were charged with several accounts of grand theft, possession of stolen goods, assault, etc. No one was charged with rape because no one knew about it.

The story hit the front page in the Star-Times and went national on the wire services. Jennifer did her best to report to the public the outrages committed on The Farm's wealthy seniors. She was certain the thieves would be put away for a long time.

Paul was, as Lana predicted, highly useful in their capture. But he, like the others, was shocked by Bob's suicide. Paul sent an officer to report it to Lana and J.P. immediately after they found Bob.

When Friday opened the door to see a uniformed officer there she started shaking all over again.

"Sorry, miss. May I please speak to Lana Koppler and J.P. Stein?"

"We're in here officer," Lana, now fully dressed and reinforced with the courage her laced tea brought her, was seated in her favorite brocaded blue Wing chair. Usually that color complimented her eyes. Not today. Both were blackened from bruises. She waved him in.

"I've really bad news."

Lana asked him to sit down, but he declined.

"Mr. Casey asked me to come here. They are wrapping up the investigation but they found Mr. Redding had hung himself in his apartment."

"What!" Lana's shout was so loud J.P. feared for her friend. Two shocks of such magnitude so close together might just be too much. J.P. also felt the pang of a déjà vu moment, remembering her own uncle's suicide as a child and her college friend.

"Officer please sit down and tell us what you know," J.P. pleaded.

The officer sat down, accepted Friday's cup of coffee, then detailed how they broke into Bob apartment and found him hanging in his home office. The officer told them many stolen items were on his desk ready to be packed up to send and on the desk was his airline ticket to Europe.

Before Lana could ask, he added, "There also was a painting of some sort. My lieutenant unwrapped part of it and commented on what a lovely frame it had."

"I knew It. I knew it," Lana said softly, mostly to herself, but audible. But then, clearly and out loud, she asked herself, "Why did he do that to me?"

J.P. tried to help her dear friend assimilate all that was happening. "Lana, you said in those early years Bob was a good guy, a super intellect, one who carefully planned almost every move of his life. Everything worked for him up until now. When this plan failed, he apparently chose death over humiliation."

Lana took the ever-present brandy on the coffee table that was in a fancy crystal decanter and decided to pour it out straight into another glass, drank it despite the early hour. The others declined after Lana offered a tall one to them. J.P. looked at Lana and feared for her friend's life that day.

"Lana are you alright? Would you like to go lie down?"

But Lana waved Jennifer off.

"My God, no, J.P. Had Bob been arrested he would have gone to prison for a long time, I'm sure. Perhaps in his warped mind, suicide was a better choice. We all have choices, you know. I've known Bob for a long time and never would I have thought he'd end up like this." A small sob did escape.

The police officer arose. "I'm sorry to bring this news to you ladies. I must go now and return to my team. "

Friday was quickly at the door before him, opening it.

J.P. and Lana sat silently in the living room for several minutes, absorbing the news. Finally, Lana asked, "I wonder what happened to Jim?"

Paul came by shortly and filled both of them in on him.

"Jim's locked up as is that security guard who broke into your apartment Lana and roughed you up. He, and a few of his cohorts he named were also arrested, including guards on Bob's security team. They all will get stiff sentences."

Paul intensified his look first at Lana, with her bruised face, then back to J.P, and felt it was time to question them both a bit more. But J.P. shook her head no. They still could read each other's thoughts. J.P. said out loud she'd go now and call in her story. To Paul she sent a telepathic message; let's just leave it at that.

Later Paul told Jennifer the other law enforcement officers and police thanked him for his help, then left. Paul gave them what he knew from his years reporting and living abroad. One member of Lana's private detective team said he'd be in touch with her when Lana felt better.

Paul did reveal that Jim had held out on Bob. He had in his possession a lot of jewelry, apparently never turned over to Bob. Police also found a beautiful diamond ring set, later returned to Mary after she came down and identified it. Others did the same.

Other small jewelry attributed to Jim's sticky fingers and found in his possession had no immediate owners. Jim maintained these were all gifts to him, but much later proved to be "lifts" he stole from his admiring female wealthy fans from various affairs.

Jim was true to form, Paul told J.P. He had such an inflated love affair going with himself that he thought he could do no wrong and soon would be released. Women pampered and gifted him all the time so he didn't have to steal, he asserted. Police didn't buy it. But Jim maintained he was not a thief, rather a paid escort who was often rewarded for services rendered. Paul told J.P. that Jim denied any knowledge of a plan to hurt or kill Lana, even though Bob suspected she was aware of their master plan. Bob was also intent on silencing Wayne Richardson.

Under intense questioning Jim told officers Bob felt Wayne Richardson was about to blow the whistle on their master plan before it could be executed. So Bob had sent his enforcer to Wayne's apartment to scare him into silence.

The guard told Bob he'd been persuasive to Wayne that day and assured him Wayne Richardson wouldn't be blowing the whistle of anyone ever again. Under intense questioning police got a confession by that security guard followed that he's roughed up Wayne and when he collapsed, left him to die. J.P. who in her gut knew this, felt vindicated.

Jennifer later interviewed Carolyn after the news had died down a bit.

"I knew something wasn't quite right. A lot of those big donors' checks meant for WOLD I never saw. I had no idea of how much people had contributed. But in order to get WOLD up and running I agreed to Bob's terms at everyone's expense, especially mine," Carolyn told J.P.

She added, "I've told you that Jim on air was a treasure. People loved him and his stories. They were better than reading about him. In some way they became invested in his colorful lifestyle. Now I see him as a Jekyll and Hyde."

"Jim was a committed lifetime big spender," I reminded her. "When his funds went south, he turned criminal. He specifically came to The Farm not to retire, but to plunder. Bob invited him to be in on his big theft at The Farm. That evidence Lana and Wayne had that would have incriminated Bob and Jim disappeared. They were not found."

* * *

Later The Farm's vice president was put in charge of the retirement community. Station manager Carolyn became the executive director of WOLD, with the buck to stop at her door, literally and figuratively. She was given command of all WOLD finances. "I have so many donors to thank," she told J.P.

What surprised Jennifer was Bob's suicide. Always a star, he could not face up to the humiliation of being caught as a criminal. The media that Bob so hated, from stories generated by J.P. and her peers, swept over the pristine Farm's campus. That presence alone could have given Bob a heart attack, had he not taken his own life. He was a top planner for years; never in his entire career had he imagined he'd be caught.

Once Jennifer's story broke about the international ring of jewelry and art thieves on the campus of The Farm, it was big news worldwide. The gang was well known internationally, but its members, so far, were never identified or caught. But with Bob's death and Jim's arrest, at least two associates became news.

Jennifer broke the story first as an exclusive. It became the story of her life, at least so far.

Trish, once she recovered from the possible danger that story brought on to all, demanded her mother fill her in on all the details as to what Lana's penthouse looked like.

As an art major in college, she had to ask, "Mom, where is that fabulous art collection of Lana's? I'd love to see her originals."

"Honey, I'm afraid that won't ever happen. I know you love art and perhaps someday soon she'll invite you to her place with me. But Lana will never reveal where the originals are. We are friends but she hasn't lived ninety years by revealing her secrets. She's Lana, sometimes even a benevolent dictator when it comes to protecting what's hers."

Trish was comfortable with the thought that perhaps soon she'd actually see the inside of that fabulous penthouse for herself.

Then Trish's thoughts turned to the budding relationship between her mother and Paul. She didn't actually need her Mom to tell her anything out loud. The happiness on J.P.'s face whenever Paul was around told it all.

Still, one day Trish had to ask, "So, Mom, what's the next big story you want to cover?" She knew news was in her mother's DNA as a personal and incurable disease. But J.P. replied, "I need a break first – and soon."

How did The Farm retirement community thrive through and after this scandal? It absorbed the shock, thankful that all the crimes were solved.

J.P. reported in her follow up stories there wasn't much of a turnover in The Farm's resident population, as Bob had feared there might be if any negative news ever leaked out. Superficially he had protected The Farm, but actually he was there to set up and plunder its wealth.

One thing J.P. lauded him for was his longtime belief that exercise was critical to a good old age.

In spite of his criminal intent, Bob did care about making The Farm a role model institution for elders of the future. In that effort he'd succeeded. Other retirement communities began plans to mimic what The Farm and Bob Redding already provided, ways to stay fit into old age.

Actually, for many of its affluent residents, the scandal was more of a turn on instead of a turn off and did not create an exodus from Pleasant Hill Farm. Some residents told J.P. they actually liked being associated with headline news.

So there was no panic, no mass move-outs. J.P. reported in her stories she had great admiration for The Farm's elders. She reported, "These seniors didn't get to such grand old ages by being weak or frightened. Many of them had survived serious conflicts and turmoil in their long lifetimes. Some encountered police and criminals. None moved out because of the scandal and Bob's suicide.

Carolyn Armstrong at WOLD was shocked to find out about the extent of criminal acts committed by Bob and Jim. But as a byproduct Carolyn experienced moments of fame, as she was first to report live on WOLD radio the scandal as it happened, right along with her corps of beloved elder volunteers.

J.P. witnessed and reported on one hilarious scene during the crisis inside WOLD studios. Several self-appointed senior reporters, all volunteers, rushed in and out to bring Carolyn, who was on air, all the latest news and residents' opinions.

One senior "reporter" got her picture in the paper. She wore a Fedora hat with what appeared to be a press pass in its hatband. Carolyn told J.P. the woman remembered that old movie with Rosalind Russell in "His Girl Friday" where male reporters wore hats.

Carolyn asked her, "Where in the world did you get that hat?"

The woman told Carolyn, "It was my late husband's hat. I thought since we've became WOLD reporters, I should look like one."

Despite the tragedy of Bob's suicide and the other events, that Rosalind Russell reference brought a light moment to the chaos that spilled over the campus that day.

It was Carolyn who kept little WOLD on air around the clock doing its big news and just after. A first for WOLD who by Carolyn's instructions did not do news. Now she planned as its executive director and general manager she would carry local news along with her senior programming. She also told J.P., "This station will make money. I also see into the future other radio stations broadcasting from inside other senior communities across the nation. But remember, we were first."

J.P. was told Carolyn also was up for a national award for broadcasting on air throughout the scandal and the drama at The Farm, the criminals and deaths, plus the big robbery that was foiled. She'd get her wish for WOLD to get its first award.

WOLD was now known as the little FM station that survived trauma and thrived. No local big FM stations now would force it out of business. Sponsors flocked to the studios to get their commercials on air.

Its music format was fine-tuned a bit by Carolyn to include news and special programming of interest to mature adults. Its survival also was assured by a hefty donation WOLD received anonymously put directly into Carolyn's hands by an attorney, which put the station in good financial shape as well.

Jennifer suspected it was Lana who dumped some of her plentiful cash into WOLD's coffers, insuring its long-term success. Lana loved those crazy seniors who knew how to roll with the punches, and throw a few themselves.

So life at The Farm would go on. Many more affluent and active seniors moved in, assuring its success. Some came, Jennifer suspected, because they were titillated by living in such a newsworthy place. But once there, she was sure they found it retirement paradise.

There were no more robberies. The manure at the Farm was permanently removed. The Farm had become a national role model for all retirement communities. Its active format forced boards of directors at other places to re-think how seniors in the future would want to live and love in retirement.

The scandal did, at least locally, also lift that veil of invisibility that for decades in America shrouded seniors' lives. Now others saw Farm residents as lively, informative, active and even sexy.

Mary continued on as Lana's bridge partner at gossip central, often wearing both her engagement and wedding rings.

True friends who had suffered greatly from the crisis, both Mary and Lana vowed to make Lana's 100th birthday party in 1986 the biggest one ever. Lana promised Mary she'd will herself to live that long and, knowing Lana, Mary and everyone else believed it.

WOLD's senior volunteers, the public discovered, would still be involved in society, not shun it. They would continue to exercise, be of service to others and to be productive during all of their lives, not just some of their lives, and for as long as their lives lasted.

The Farm proved, too, that sometimes-bad notoriety could help promote good results, such as the new popularity of The Farm's active lifestyle for seniors.

Best of all, The Farm's main attraction, WOLD, saw its volunteer corps double.

Many WOLD listeners sent in checks to help support its music format and keep it on air.

Listeners old and new realized that the little FM radio voice heralded old age as an adventure, not a downer. Actually **WOLD** was preaching that as gospel. Its programs reassured listeners that "golden" as in the golden years didn't mean wealth, but rather the richness that comes from shared experiences.

At least that's how Jennifer ended her last big story, adding **WOLD** and its founder Carolyn Armstrong would continue to profile seniors and give them new ways to successfully age.

Stories on The Farm in the Star-Times also cemented Jennifer's job security at the Star-Times. Other than mentioning Lana's painting and jewels as the key to breaking the case, nothing was ever written about the vicious rape Lana suffered. It remains the secret Lana and Jennifer would share until their deaths.

In all her reporting years, Jennifer had promised herself always to report the crime of rape, and get rapists arrested. But this time she went silent, for Lana's sake. So the guy got away with it. But when much later on after his confession and charged with Wayne Richardson's death, she felt justice was mostly served.

Lana recovered completely. If she could bottle what it is in her constitution that makes her so strong at ninety, J.P. thought, Lana could make still another fortune selling it.

Lana told J.P. her plan to throw that big bash on her 100th birthday stating it would become the party of the century. J.P. was sure it would and vowed to be there.

Never missing a beat, Lana also gave Paul and J.P. a grand dinner party after they announced both were leaving together for Paris soon for a decades-postponed vacation.

In the weeks that followed the scandal, Paul and J. P. were almost inseparable. "How about we hop a plane real soon for Paris and see that big city together?" he proposed, trying to duplicate his first proposition to her decades ago at the end of their senior year in college.

Co-habitate? "Why thank you, I'd love it. Would tomorrow be too soon?"

J.P. had told Lana privately that she and Paul were pragmatists about their new relationship in middle age.

She told Lana, "We will go for as long as it takes to re-acquaint ourselves with each other, in every delicious possible way. Then sooner rather than later we will decide if we also have a future together."

"How long will you be in Paris?" Lana asked. "And while there, will you and Paul sign 'I do' papers? That's what I'm hoping for."

J.P. didn't answer her directly. Instead she just smiled, hugged her dear friend, and whispered into her ear the words that best identified Lana behavior: "Isn't it true that whatever Lana wants, Lana always gets?"

Epilogue

That little fire of 1976 at The Farm was dwarfed by a true emergency that hit the campus in 1986 one night after Lana's 100th birthday party. Not exactly a tornado, but high winds did a lot of damage. No one in that Farm suburb had lights, heat or deliveries.

Senior occupants turned into heroes, helping each other escape, find food and survive a week without utilities. One resident, a woman in a wheelchair in a plush apartment on the first floor, turned her patio grill, propane heated, into a soup kitchen. Others brought fresh and frozen foods about to spoil to utilize since there was no refrigeration, to flavor the huge pot. Mrs. Ratz's exotic soups were passed around freely.

Many seniors remembered the Great Depression of the 1930s in Cincinnati when as children they witnessed soup kitchens all over the city to help feed the homeless and hopeless.

Lana Koppler proved once again, not only her strong survival instincts, but a true friend when there is a need. She helped serve meals, check on residents to make sure they were well and got them needed medications.

The night before that emergency happened Farm residents were invited to Lana's 100th birthday party. Entertainers came in from all over America to honor her. It seemed someone in every part of the country benefited from her generosity.

"May I have this dance, Mrs. Koppler?"

The tall gentleman bent over to Lana, taking her hand.

"Senator, I'd be honored."

The orchestra Lana hired sensed a moment in time, slowed the rhythm and the floor emptied.

"What do you think you did that allowed you to live to 100 as such a remarkable, able, and agile woman?"

"Senator, you flatter me. My agility is grossly overrated."

"I hear you climb five flights of stairs often for fitness sake."

"More like for God's sake, I'm not dead yet."

His laugh was not only loud, it was infectious.

"I do hope I'll reach 100 and will be as active as you."

"Senator, I didn't plan it, it just happened. And if you take me around the dance floor one more time, I'll not reach 101."

The Senator returned Lana to her seat at the head of a long table, piled not with gifts at her request, but with letters, cards, and many donations to her favorite charities.

One pile of donations was in response to an interview Lana had just two weeks before her 100th birthday party on WOLD.

Carolyn Armstrong, executive director of WOLD, asked Lana for one significant remembrance from her past.

Lana replied, "The day I fired my women's literary club."

"Why? What happened?"

"We had scheduled a special program that day. Our program chairwoman had heard of a black child prodigy pianist who at age six, could play without music, the works of all the classics from Mozart to Beethoven. It was just before the start of World War II in the thirties. It was a high tea event."

"What upset you?"

"Small for her age, the child needed some additional cushioning for the piano bench. Our chairwoman set it up. There was great anticipation for the event. Then as the final prop, the chairwoman placed a three-panel screen in front of the piano where the girl would be. Many gasped. Some were upset. They wouldn't be able to see the performer."

"That was unusual. What did you do?"

"I got up and walked over to the chairwoman and asked her to remove it immediately. The audience must see the performer."

Lana said then that chairwoman whispered into her ear, 'Lana, she's colored. Many members said they were offended that I'd even engaged a Negro performer for our tea, famous or not. So as not to offend those who would be by having a Negro perform at their event, I decided with their approval to put a screen in front of the girl. The members won't see her, only hear her. Our members approved."

Lana fumed, told that chairwoman, "If you don't immediately take that screen way before that child sees it, I will resign my membership and withdraw financial support of this organization. And you never will appear in any of my future events as my guests. You are all considered fired."

Lana added they didn't remove the screen. So Lana walked out.

Much later, Lana said, she asked the child and her mother to her mansion to perform for her guests.

"How was she?" Carolyn asked.

"Magnificent."

Lana told Carolyn she not only hated cheats and liars, but bigots as well.

Carolyn retold that story at Lana's memorial. She said that event defined Lana Koppler for who she was.

The Lana Koppler memorial service occurred two months after Lana's 100th birthday party; she'd passed away in her sleep.

That child prodigy became a famous concert pianist. So at Lana's memorial she once again performed for her deceased friend. It was Lana's big donation in her will to The Farm recently that insured the now famous pianist would, at her retirement, become The Farm's first black resident.

* * *